THE MANY FACES OF ROBERT MARSHALL

Written

By

ROBERT MITCHELL

This is a work of fiction. All names, characters, and settings are fictitious. Any resemblance to actual events, names, locales, organizations, or persons living or dead, is entirely coincidental.

Chapter 1

Everett Gentry was sitting listening to the crackling sounds coming from the fire. He looked at the other men seated around it, he could just make out their faces in the flickering light. They, like him, were scared of what would happen to them tomorrow, for at first light they would attack the confederate army. It was May 2, 1863, this was going to be known as the second battle of Fredericksburg in Virginia. Eleven hundred union soldiers would be dead after the battle, and Everett Gentry was going to be amongst them. He sat full of life that night, joking and laughing, and began thinking about his mother and father. He was a farm boy from Ohio, and longed to return home. He thought of his mother's cooking and longed for those days. He had a girl at home waiting for him, she was beautiful, tall with black hair and the greenest eyes, he thought of her as he sat and listened. One of the men Everett knew only as Stinky, for obvious reasons, had a juice harp and began playing. Some of the men started slapping spoons on spoons, and this makeshift little band helped calm the nerves of the men. He slept near that fire, wrapped in a wool army blanket. It would be the same blanket that she would wrap his body in after the battle. The lead ball entered Everett's chest, and he could remember the feeling well. The large caliber ball had left the gun barrel of a confederate soldier and Everett thought he had been kicked by a horse. He lay in the mud on the battlefield and then he saw her, she appeared from nowhere and came towards him. He thought for a moment it was his girl from back home, he was certain that he was already dead, but she turned him over and he realized he must be hallucinating. It was his girl, she was beautiful beyond belief, but her eyes, were not the green eyes he knew so well. He had stared at these eyes, and noticed they were each a different colour, she told him not to worry, everything was going to be alright, and as he stared at her mismatched eyes she said, "I promise we will meet again, someday." He then heard a strange noise. It was bells, he heard the ringing of bells. His final thought as he closed his eyes was, am I going to heaven?

Robert reached for the alarm clock, he still used it only because it had been a gift from his late Father. It was an old mechanical wind with two bells on top and a small hammer that was loud enough to wake the dead. He opened his eyes and looked around his small apartment. It took a moment for him to realize that it was just a dream,

Robert should not have been surprised. The dreams began while recovering from an automobile accident, close to a year earlier. The strange dreams had stopped shortly after leaving the hospital, just as his Doctor had predicted, but for the forty-seven year old Robert Marshall the recurrence of these dreams allowed him to visit past lives. They were his own past lives that were supposed to remain buried, but his accident had changed that, and now he was about to meet the woman who appeared in these dreams.

The accident had happened as he was driving his mother and father to the airport on their yearly trip to Florida. The roads were clear, with the exception of one drunk driver, who was returning from an all-nighter. He had crossed in front of Robert on a two lane road at precisely the wrong time. Robert had struck his head on the dash of the car during that accident, and found himself lying in a hospital bed, tubes and wires connected him to machines that monitored his brain function. He was in a coma, but his brain was still functioning. Doctor Biggles was studying a chart with brain activity, and didn't see the nurse enter the room. She had looked at the chart earlier, and asked Doctor Biggles if he had ever seen a person's brain activity look like that. Doctor Biggles was surprised by her entrance, and blurted out, "What do you mean, nurse?" "I'm sorry Doctor I didn't mean to startle you, I just meant that the patient has no brain activity for a certain amount of time each and every day, if I didn't know better I would think that his brain died and then miraculously came back to life." "The equipment is obviously faulty then, isn't it?" said a somewhat bothered looking Dr. Biggles. "I'm sorry for the outburst nurse, I just found a loose wire, and am certain that is the likely problem." The nurse went about with her usual routine. She checked the patients' temperature, changed a fluids bag and moved on to another patient. Dr. Biggles waited until the door closed to the private room of Robert Marshall before he spoke. "Robert, listen to me carefully, I know you can hear me. You need to wake up, you need to wake up now!" Robert's eyes began to flutter, and as he left his comatose state, he returned to the world in which he belonged. Doctor Biggles was relieved to see the patient open his eyes. He really wasn't looking forward to killing Robert if he didn't have to, but he was sworn to keep his secret safe and keep the general population in the dark. Robert opened his eyes and looked at Dr. Biggles. He noticed that the good doctor was of slight build, and most likely of East Indian decent. He smiled at Robert, and Robert smiled back. Still, something about the Doctor was familiar to Robert, he had seen him before, he was certain of that.

Robert looked at the Doctor and asked him a question. "Where am I?" Doctor Biggles had a stern look on his face as he spoke. "You are in the hospital, and have been in a coma for the last ten days, do you remember what happened?" "I remember driving my parents to the airport." Robert stopped, and then continued, "Where are my parents? Are they alright?" Doctor Biggles didn't want to shock the patient, at least not yet. "Don't you worry about them, you have to get yourself better first." Robert would later learn that both of his parents were pronounced dead at the scene, and now, with them gone, he was totally alone. Sure, he had a few friends arrive for visits, but he had no siblings, and an ex-wife that could have cared less. She did come to see him once, while he was still in a coma, but she did not come back after he regained consciousness. The strange dreams that he had while in the coma had started a short time later while he was still recovering in the hospital. He was certain he had killed his parents. "If only we had not stopped at the local coffee shop," he said to his doctor, with tears filling his eyes. His parents didn't want to stop, but Robert loved his coffee too much. The stop placed them on a collision course that Robert felt was entirely his doing. Doctor Biggles didn't agree. "Stop beating yourself up, it was an accident, and accidents do happen whether we want them to or not." Robert told Doctor Biggles that he was having very strange dreams. The dreams, he thought, belonged to other people, and he had somehow hijacked them. The dreams were someone else's life condensed into one night and experienced in vivid colour for him to relive. His dreams all ended the same way, with that person's death and Robert waking up. His doctor told him that he should not worry about dreams. "You must remember Robert that you received a rather nasty bump on the head, and some strange dreams may be part of that injury." Robert had strange dreams night after night, and when he left the hospital to return to his apartment, he was hoping the dreams would stop. He continued his recovery at home, and as the doctor had predicted, the dreams began to subside and eventually vanish completely. He had been home for several months and had been able to slowly return part -time to his job as a telemarketer. He had one final check up with Dr. Biggles, and if everything seemed normal he was told he could resume a full schedule. Robert waited not so patiently for that day to arrive, he wanted so desperately get on with his life.

Chapter 2

The day arrived as they always do, and Robert was hoping to see Dr. Biggles for the last time. Robert waited patiently for his appointment time, he was sitting looking through the magazines in the waiting area. He really wasn't paying any attention to his surroundings. He was doing the same thing everybody does, he was flipping the pages, not really reading, just doing something to pass the time. He had the strange feeling that someone was watching him. He looked around at the others waiting in that room, but to his surprise nobody was looking at him. He again looked back at his magazine, but he couldn't shake the feeling. He again looked up from his magazine, and his eyes stopped on the girl at the reception desk. She was looking at him, but immediately looked away when his eyes caught hers. He had the same weird feeling he had when he saw Dr. Biggles for the first time. He was certain he had met this girl before. She was not the usual woman on reception, and as he continued to stare at her she stood, walked out of his line of sight, and he then heard the sound of a door closing. He returned to flipping pages, and didn't look up again until his name was called. He placed the book on a side table and approached the reception desk. He stopped dead in his tracks and stared at the woman on reception who had just called his name. She wasn't the same girl he had seen earlier, this woman was much older, and he suddenly realised that this was the lady he had seen on his previous visits. Robert blurted out, "Excuse me, but has the other receptionist gone for the day?" "I am Dr. Biggles only receptionist I have been with him for ten years." Robert was suddenly wondering if his mind was playing tricks on him, and as he entered the examination room, the doctor could see that he had something on his mind. "You look like a man who has just seen a ghost," said Dr. Biggles. Robert sat down and proceeded to tell the doctor of his recent encounter with the receptionist. "I looked up from my book and saw a lady staring at me from the desk, I believed that I knew this person from somewhere, but didn't know where." "You think you have seen my receptionist before, but you have, you saw her at our last appointment," said Biggles. "The lady that I saw today was not the receptionist, but someone else. I asked the receptionist where she had gone, and she had no idea who I was talking about," said a now distraught Robert. "Can you describe this woman to me," asked Dr. Biggles. "She was in her mid - thirties black hair, very attractive and there was something strange about her eyes," said Robert. Dr. Biggles had no idea who Robert had seen in the office, he asked Robert a number of questions meant to evaluate his recovery before giving Robert the nod to return to full activities. "No more dreams where you believe you are someone else?" asked Dr. Biggles. "No, now if I have a dream, I really don't remember. Maybe bits and pieces. I dreamed the other night about a girl," said Robert. Dr. Biggles smiled "maybe it was the girl you saw in my office." "No, I don't think it was the girl I saw today, I really think we have met before, maybe in a previous life," answered Robert. "Many people believe in déjà vu, but I am not so sure about previous life experiences," said a now more sombre Dr. Biggles as he continued, "you have more than likely seen this woman before, and you don't remember." "I guess you're right Doc, I may have passed her on the street, on the way to work, or seen her in a store somewhere," countered Robert. "Exactly," said Dr. Biggles. "Now Robert I think that you can return to work on a full time basis. Remember if you get headaches or grow tired easily, you are doing too much, and you don't want to have a relapse." Robert shook the Doctor's hand as he thanked him, and as he started to leave the office Dr. Biggles said one more thing to Robert. "Promise me one thing," said the doctor to his patient, "if those strange dreams you were experiencing in the hospital return, let me know as soon as possible, as that might be an indication of a possible problem." "OK, I will let you know if I have any problems, but I am confident that I am better, thanks for your concern." Robert closed the door on his way out, and as soon as he had, Dr. Biggles walked over to a different door and invited the woman in. She entered, sat down and spoke. "Well, do you think we have anything to worry about Ben?" Dr. Ben Biggles looked at the woman for a moment before he spoke. "He may be a problem for us, but I'm just not certain yet," said Biggles. "Maybe we should discuss it with the council," said the attractive black haired woman with two different coloured eyes. "No, not yet, he is getting better and he is not having the dreams, so for now I suggest that we keep an eye on him, he hasn't exposed us, and if the dreams return we can bring it to their attention then." "You are in charge Ben, do you have any orders for me?" asked the woman with the condition known as heterochromia. "Stay away from him, and wear your contact lenses, if he sees you again it may trigger the dreams, and we can't have that, can we?" She stood in front of Dr. Biggles and gave him the customary hand salute. She opened the door and as she stepped through the threshold she vanished into thin air. Doctor Biggles didn't even raise an eyebrow as he watched her disappear, instead he called the receptionist and asked for his next patient.

Robert, following his doctors' orders resumed his usual boring life. He couldn't however forget about the woman he had seen at the reception desk. He started to find himself dreaming of her. "How could I be so obsessed over a woman I have never met?" He said out loud as he sat at a coffee shop with his friend Roy Summerset. Roy was an American Indian who Robert had met and befriended at the call center. Roy had started work at the center while Robert was convalescing at home. They became fast friends, and soon the two were spending considerable time together. Roy asked, "are you sure you haven't seen her before, and you just don't remember?" "I don't think so, but I'm not certain, you see I have been dreaming of her, but I can't remember much, in the dream she is smiling at me and I keep thinking about those eyes." "Tell me what you remember about her eyes," said Roy. "I don't know, maybe it's nothing," said Robert to his now very inquisitive friend, and then he continued, "they were different colours, I think," "Really, you sure?" asked Roy. "No, I don't know, it was just a dream, can we talk about something else?" asked Robert. "Yes, we can talk about something else, but you worry me, you sure you aren't having those strange dreams that you told me about earlier?" asked Roy. "No, nothing like that, those dreams have vanished," said Robert. Roy smiled at his friend and told him he would see him tomorrow. Roy left the table walked outside and down the street, he walked a considerable distance before he turned the corner, and as he did, he disappeared into thin air. He was now waiting in the dark, and when the door opened he stepped into the office of Dr. Biggles. "Hello Roy, give me your report," said the good doctor. "He is still dreaming of Cassandra, I don't think she should have appeared here for him to see; I think she should stay away from him," said Roy. "I have spoken with her, and she gave me her word that she would not let him see her again," said a stern sounding Dr. Biggles. "Can she be trusted, she seems to be drawn to this man, said a concerned Roy. "Maybe it is time to go to the council." "No, we do not need to alert the others at this time, you just need to be with him, he trusts you, remember, his parents have died and he doesn't have anyone else to talk to. We don't want him spreading any crazy ideas to others in the general population," said Dr. Biggles. "We don't want him spreading the truth, isn't that what you really mean?" countered Roy. "We must remain in the background, as we have for countless centuries, we owe it to the original MAN civilization." Roy was fully aware of what had happened in the past. "I will continue to monitor Robert Marshall, and send him here if anything changes," and with that remark Roy stood, saluted again and walked to the door he had entered earlier. He was on his way through when receptionist Joyce Goldblum opened the door. She saw him vanish as he entered the closet, and with mouth open in amazement she turned to Dr. Biggles. He had no choice, he disappeared as well. Joyce fainted and dropped to the floor, and Dr. Biggles rematerialized a few seconds later. He walked over to Joyce and propped her up. Joyce opened her eyes and stared at Dr. Biggles. "Oh, Ben, what happened to me?" "I don't know Joyce, you entered the room, and just collapsed on the floor. Maybe we should run some tests?" Joyce sat for a moment, she was trying to comprehend what she had really witnessed. Ben Biggles was still cradling her head. She looked at him, he hadn't vanished so she must have imagined the whole thing. "I am alright now, but I think I need to get my eyes checked," she said with conviction. Dr. Biggles helped her to her feet and suggested she go home and get a good night sleep, and he would see her tomorrow. Joyce left the office, and although she really had seen both men in that office disappear her mind would not accept the truth. This was something the twelve Huelowen's, who made up the council, could always count on. The human population, for the most part, never wants to believe that anything strange is occurring. The ones that do, the people who believe they have had previous lives, or seen ghosts, are ridiculed. Some are still not swayed to give up the notion, and then the council has no other choice than to eliminate them. Dr. Biggles didn't like that word, it had a finality to it, but to the Huelowen's it meant rebirth. Each human life on the planet continued, forever. The deceased was immediately starting a new life as an infant, with no memories of the previous life, but sometimes people did remember a previous life, and that could be best handled by no interaction with that person by anyone on the council. Friends and family would laugh it off, and in the media they would be ridiculed or possibly called crazy. The system worked well, but it did have some floaters. The council called them that, and Robert Marshall may still become one, he had seen a few of his previous lives after his head injury, and if he were to continue dreaming of a different life that he had experienced he would be considered a floater, and would be a danger to all humans, if more of them were to believe their dreams then they too would become floaters themselves. It was therefore the responsibility of the council to police the humans, and not allow them to discover who they really were. Human scientists continue to dig through the ancient ruins of early civilizations looking for clues as to where they came from, and this was the most troubling and tiresome aspect of the council's job. Human's, it turns out, are a most inquisitive creature, and won't stop digging for clues about the past. This was something that the Huelowen's had not anticipated when they arrived on earth and bred with the MAN civilization more than five thousand years earlier.

Chapter 3

The Huelowen were an advanced race of biped people. They had built space craft to explore the vast regions of space, and finding no life on any of the nearby planets, they decided to explore deeper into space. These early flights, and the toll they took on the crews led to some drastic action. Scientists had been working on gene modification as a way to hopefully extend the lives of future space travellers, and over the next hundred years made great advancements in this field. The next set of space explorers did indeed grow old more slowly, and the process was expanded to the general population. The scientists had stumbled onto the gene sequence that would change their world forever. Huelowen's now were reaching adulthood and did not appear to be aging. Great celebrations were held for the scientists responsible, they had inadvertently created something that later would come back to haunt them, immortality. The returning astronauts had being studying a planet outside of their own solar system, and discovered advanced civilizations on one planet, it was the third planet from the sun, and the Huelowen's named it Man 3. They landed and after further investigation realized that the inhabitants of the planet were very similar in appearance to themselves, but not nearly as advanced as previously thought. They would not return to the planet for the next two hundred years. In that time they realized as the population grew on their home planet, people were not dying. They were going to have to make some difficult choices. Although they believed that they were immortal, this was not an entirely true statement. They still required food and water, if they had these things they aged at a rate that could not be measured with any degree of accuracy. The Huelowen's solution was a drastic one. They must sterilize the entire male population. To some, this was not acceptable, and a motion was put forward to the council to shift some of the population to the newly discovered MAN 3. The council decided against such action, pending further studies. It was at this time that one of the scientists came up with a solution of his own. He would chemically sterilize small parts of the population, and report on the results. The sterilization project was well received by the participants in the study. They believed that once the drug was removed from the system they would return to a reproductive state. This new proposal was met with optimism, and as the results were made available to the council it became clear that the study group should be expanded. The scientist who had developed this chemical compound unfortunately had ulterior motives. His belief was that the Huelowen had become an abomination, and must be stopped at all costs. The plan he had devised was, in his mind, necessary. The compound was developed by several scientists, and his was the final step before release to the public. The compound would be added to the water source, as this was the easiest way to administer it. What the other scientists were unaware of was that, after the initial tests were complete, one more ingredient was added. This additive's only function was to coat the stomach wall with a blocking agent, and that agent would stop the absorption of nutrients from food. The person would then starve to death. In the Huelowen it would take several years for the effects to be seen, and by then it would be too late. The council, maybe by luck more than design, chose to separate out a small percentage of the population from receiving this compound. The council, scientists and astronauts were selected first, and then one area was selected at random. Once the compound was released into the water source it was too late, the effects of the coating compound could not be reversed. It required several years for the effects of one lone scientist to be realized, and when the other scientists discovered the modified compound in the water, that scientist was brought before the council.

"You have been charged with a crime against the Huelowen people. How do you plead?" asked the council. The scientist known as Hades looked down at the floor. "I am guilty, none of us should live forever, it's wrong to believe we are something that we are not." He then concluded his statement with the following remark, "you need not worry yourselves with my punishment for I have already swallowed enough compound to ..." He dropped to the floor in front of the council and as he lay dying he smiled a sick smile, and he was gone. The council now was left to inform those citizens treated that they had been poisoned by one rogue scientist, how much longer they would live was unknown. The scientist had hinted that he had contaminated all water sources on the planet, but testing proved otherwise. It was only a small temporary victory, the source of untreated water would be exhausted in less than twenty years. Immediately, a ship was readied for the long trip to Man 3. The council had instructed them to land at ten well defined civilizations, ones that had been mapped out on a previous mission and collect several of the biped beings from each location, both male and female would be required for experiments that hopefully could help save the Huelowen race. The council members were busy during this time overseeing the construction of larger spacecraft to make the trip to MAN 3. They were out of options, the population was dying, and riots were prevalent. They hoped that they would be able to co-exist with the indigenous biped, when the spacecraft returned they learned several important things, the species was a close relative, much closer than previously thought, and were of a similar size and build, and that breeding with them would be possible. However, the most amazing thing happened purely by accidental contact. The Huelowen scientist touched the visitor without wearing gloves, and almost instantly his skin colour changed to match that of the species. Huelowen's had a grey greenish tint to their skin, and now several of them were brown. This camouflage reaction would allow the Huelowen's to blend in to each society. They had collected these people from different continents, and kept them separated. The Huelowen's scientists, after studying all of the data, realized that these people had spread from a single source across the planet, and had in the process created offspring of many mixed races. The fourteen spacecraft were ready for departure, each one headed for their respective zone. Each Huelowen on board now looked very similar in appearance to the indigenous species that they were hoping to blend with. The voyage was well planned, the ship would drop its payload in the region and then scuttle the craft in the ocean. They were never expecting a return flight, this was a one way mission, and the craft could never be found by inhabitants of MAN 3. The council had been increased in size to fourteen members, one member on each craft, with the hopes that if a problem were to arise on any one vessel the council would not be entirely lost. The scientists studying MAN 3 found that large bodies of water covered much of the planet. Probes dropped into that water proved to be very useful. Some of the areas proved to be very deep, and it was in these locations that the spent ships would be deposited.

The flight was not without disaster. The convoy lost two ships on route to the new planet. The remainder of the ships dropped their cargo in predetermined locations. They were in close proximity to these advanced civilizations, with the hope that they would be able to slowly integrate with them over time. The remaining twelve council members met and set up council to oversee the integration. The Huelowens were never in a rush, they didn't have to be, and that patience paid off. Slowly they mingled with the population, it had been decided that only a few pregnancies would be attempted. If all went according to plan they could expand the program. The first children were born and immediately accepted, the offspring looked very much like their parents, so the plan was expanded. The council had set out some rules for the Huelowen to follow. Each Huelowen was expected to mate with the indigenous biped on the planet, and to have as many partners as possible. The council was pleased with the results. A new species was born on MAN 3, and the council decided on a new name for this species, and for this new world. The name was a combination of both worlds. The Huelowen home planet was called Earth, and to the settlers from another world this name seemed appropriate for this world, and to call these offspring Human was a lasting way to never forget where they had come from. The council would continue to meet, and although they were the governing body for the Huelowen population, to the Human race they became gods. This did not sit well with some of the Huelowen people, and over time the festering grew worse. Many of these early civilizations, with the influence of the pure Huelowens living there decided that the council was no longer needed. They were jealous of the seven male and five female council members, and only one method could be used to keep the law that had served the Huelowen so well. The mysterious compound that caused the end to many Huelowen was added to the water source of any faction opposed to council rule. Within a few short years these civilizations that had prospered for thousands of years were erased from existence, leaving nothing behind but the buildings as a reminder to others not to anger the gods. Eventually the council decided that the pure Huelowen's that were still alive should live separately from the humans they had created, and they agreed with the council findings. It became obvious over time, the benefit of a longer life diminished, when humans bred with other humans. Huelowens could no longer hide the fact that they were not aging in this changing environment. The council had found a location from prying eyes where the Huelowen could live without raising any questions of why they were not aging. This place was an island in the Atlantic, it would become known through legend as the city of Atlantis.

They did not know at that particular time that one of the effects of this breeding was continual life for the memories of the human. The human body did die, but the essence of who they were before carried on, and previous lives in fact stacked on top of one another. The Huelowen scientist's studied human patients that could recall things that had happened to them in these previous lives after waking from sleep. The scientists found in their studies that not all humans dreamed of previous lives, it only occurred when the person suffered a blow to the head or suffered a traumatic experience. The Huelowen had lived so long that they could actually confirm the dreams as reality. Furthermore, each of the studies indicated that the patient did not remain as only one sex. They may have been male or female and of many different ethnic backgrounds. It was one of the side effects of the breeding program that the scientists were unaware of, and had no scientific answers for the council when they presented their findings. The council decided that nothing needed to be done, and that most humans did not believe that the dreams were anything more than dreams.

The centuries would pass and the council was all but forgotten by the human population. They were now living amongst the humans they helped create, and would meet in a secret location directly below the Mayan ruins. The Huelowen council had lived for many lifetimes, and had acquired over that time the ability to transport themselves to any location on Earth. This teleportation worked only to places that they had physically visited in the past. Over the many millennia they also discovered that if one of members had visited a location that the others had not seen before, they could join hands with that individual and travel together. The one thing that they hadn't planned on was that this hybrid species had an interest in the unknown. Humans, it turns out, are a very inquisitive breed, and with technological advances made in the last hundred or so years, it was becoming apparent to the Huelowen's that eventually the human population would discover the past, the real past.

Chapter 4

Robert Marshall was sitting at his cubical telling some poor sucker on the other end of the line how he could help make his life better. "It was only three easy payments of nineteen ninety- five," Robert couldn't help but laugh to himself while giving his sales pitch to the man on the other end of the line. The sales pitch was a no brainer, all you needed to perform the sale was a decent voice and be able to read the computer screen with the pitch. He wasn't to chat up the buyer, just deliver the pitch. He had spoken it so many times that he barely needed to glance at his screen. On the rare occasion that he was asked something about the product the answer was already waiting, he only had to glance down the page for the appropriate answer. In the past he just did the job, but now he found the work extremely boring, almost tedious since his accident. He found himself daydreaming more, and he couldn't get that girl in the doctor's office out of his mind. Since the accident he had taken on a new hobby, painting. He had never painted before, but something inside his head told him he could paint. He purchased the necessary supplies, and set up an easel in his apartment. The first time he held the brush in his hand he knew he had painted before, he found that he could paint with an ease that frightened him. He was painting pictures of whatever entered his mind, he painted landscapes, and ships on the sea. He would no sooner finish one picture when another image popped into his head. He could see things with clarity and detail, but he had no idea where the ideas came from. He had travelled a few times with his parents when he was younger, but these images were nothing that he remembered from those trips. He then had a strange idea, he would try to paint a portrait. He had someone in mind, the beautiful girl that he seen only once in the doctor's office. He had been daydreaming about her and believed that if he started to paint her, his mind would fill in missing the pieces.

Roy Summerset was having a drink with Robert after work, he had been told to continue the surveillance, and had for the past several months not been told anything by Robert that raised flags as to his current condition. Roy did not mention the girl, nor had he heard Robert mention her. "So, anything new or exciting in your life," Roy asked. Robert had a somewhat embarrassing look on his face. "What is it? asked Roy. "Nothing really," answered Robert with a sheepish look on his face. "Come on, we're buddies, you can tell me, you don't need to be worried I won't laugh," countered Roy. "I've started painting" said Robert. "Houses?" laughed Roy. Robert stood up and walked away from Roy, he wasn't going to tell him anything else. "Hey, I'm sorry, I was just kidding," said a now apologetic Roy. "I'm heading home, I really don't need the abuse, at least not from a supposed friend," said an angry sounding Robert. "I'm sorry, I really am, so please tell me what you're painting?" asked Roy. "You really want to know? asked Robert. "Sure, I would like to see your paintings sometime," answered Roy. Robert was excited now, he really wanted to show his work and wanted an opinion. "Why not come over now, you have never been to my place." Roy had been waiting for an invitation. He wasn't really that interested in seeing Robert's paintings, but he was interested in getting inside Robert's apartment. He would only need to spend a few moments there, and then he would be able to see the location in his mind and teleport in whenever he wanted. The two arrived at the apartment, and Roy entered and sat on a couch. He was looking around and memorizing the interior, when he noticed the easel in the corner, it was covered with a white blanket. The paintings that Robert mentioned were nowhere to be seen. Roy studied the room carefully. Robert handed him a beer and proceeded to another room that Roy assumed was a bedroom. Robert returned with several paintings and as Roy looked on he realized that Robert was indeed painting from a memory of a previous life. "How long have you been painting these images?" asked a very inquisitive Roy Summerset. "I have been painting for a few weeks now, I guess," said Robert. Roy sat drinking his beer, and knew he was going to have to tell Dr. Biggles of his latest discovery. However, Roy was not ready for the picture hiding under the blanket, and when Robert removed it, Roy gasped and spilled his beer on the carpet. He should not have been surprised, he knew as soon as he saw her who she was, and although Robert had seen her only that one time in the Doctor's office, he had captured her beauty perfectly. She had been known by many names over her lifetime, Roy and the council called her Cassandra, but to the ancient Greeks she was Aphrodite. Roy was shocked, how could Robert remember her that well. "Is this the girl that you saw at your doctor's office?" asked Roy. "Yes, as I started to paint her I remembered more and more details," said Robert. Roy looked closely at the picture, and noticed that Robert had captured her eyes perfectly. "I can't believe you could paint this woman so well after seeing her just that one time," said Roy. "I can't either, however, now that I can see her picture in my apartment I have the feeling that I have known her my entire life," said Robert. "That's crazy Robert, you really believe you know her," said Roy. "I don't know, I guess not," said Robert. Roy had been in this situation before, which was one of the perks of being Huelowen. He had never seen anybody paint such a picture of Cassandra, and she would never have posed for it. People over the years had painted her from memory, and Roy remembered only one of them was accurate. The other painters had never captured her real beauty, and Roy would need to relax and not draw suspicion to himself. "I never knew you could paint this well, I'm almost speechless," said Roy. "You really think they are good, you're not just saying it," said an excited Robert. He told Roy he had not shown the paintings to anyone, and Roy smiled at him. "I have a friend who should see these paintings, his name is Edward Chow, he has an art studio in the city, are you interested?" asked Roy. "Yes, if you really think he would like to see them," said Robert. "Oh I'm certain he will want to see these, as a matter of fact why don't I call him right now and see if he is available," Roy said. Robert nodded in the affirmative, and Roy picked up the phone and after a few brief moments of conversation he hung up. While they were waiting for Mr. Chow to arrive, Roy told Robert that he had taken some art classes with Edward, "I have been studying sculpting with him, but I know he has an expert knowledge of paintings as well." The doorbell rang and Robert opened it to a slightly built older Asian gentleman. "Hello, you must be Robert, may I come in?" "Yes, please come in, may I get you something to drink?" "No thank you," he continued into the room and Roy was waiting to give proper introductions. "Thanks for coming on such short notice Edward, I would like you to meet my friend Robert Marshall," the two men shook hands and exchanged the usual pleasantries. Edward then turned to inspect the work. "Have you had any lessons?" asked Edward Chow nonchalantly. "No, I just started a few weeks ago," said a now intimidated Robert. "They are good, they are very good," Edward then turned his attention to the painting of Cassandra. He knew who she was, but he wanted to hear who Robert thought she was. "I don't know who she is I saw her only once, but I felt I had known her forever, does that make any sense?" "Yes, actually I have known many great painters, who were able to paint from their imagination." "You think I imagined her?" said a somewhat dumbfounded Robert. "Yes, I do," said Edward Chow as he continued, "I am interested in displaying all of these paintings at my gallery, I have that much confidence in your work." Robert looked at Mr. Chow for a moment, he was not really sure what to say. Roy jumped in, "of course he will consign them with you, won't you Robert?" "I guess so," said a somewhat stunned Robert. "Great, Edward I will help load them in your vehicle," said an insistent Roy. The two men wrapped the paintings and loaded them on a small trolley that Mr. Chow had brought along. Both men said good-bye to Robert and proceeded to the elevator, once inside the elevator Roy pushed the button. The door closed and the two men vanished, they immediately rematerialized in a storage room at Edward Chow's studio. Robert had no idea that Edward Chow was a Huelowen, and as such was a loyal foot soldier to the council. The population on this planet was expanding, and becoming more advanced as the centuries rolled on. The council found it necessary to enlist all remaining Huelowens to one common cause. Keep the secrets of the Huelowen civilization from the humans. It was a daunting task, and one that would eventually fail. The hope was that maybe they could contain the findings until a day when the human race would be mature enough to accept it. Edward removed the paintings from the wrap, and immediately sat the painting of the woman on an easel. "This is the best painting of Cassandra I have ever seen, you say he really only laid eyes on her once, but I don't believe it," said Edward. He then opened a door at the rear of the storage area and turned on the lights. Both men stepped inside and Roy was not surprised by the sheer number of paintings of Cassandra. He had seen them all before, and he walked over to the one that most reminded him of Robert's painting. He remembered the day he and Edward had procured it, from Leonardo da Vinci. The one Robert had just painted had similar characteristics, but Robert's showed her true eye colours. Every Huelowen had the same defect, Heterochromia, and wore contact lenses to hide that fact. "How did he know her eyes were a different colour?" asked Edward. "She wasn't wearing her contacts when he saw her at Ben's office, but Robert told me he believed he had met her somewhere before," said Roy. "It may be possible, but highly unlikely." Roy continued with orders for Edward. "Place some of his work on display and keep the rest in storage, if he comes by and I'm sure he will, he's going to ask for his mystery woman to be returned, leave the rest for me." Edward nodded and gave Roy a salute. Roy acknowledged it and then disappeared.

Roy reappeared in the closet of Ben Biggles, he was here to give a full report on his findings. The door was always closed when council members arrived, and was opened by Ben only when the coast was clear. Humans, had over the centuries, been witness to the teleportation by the Huelowen people, and these sightings would become the ghost stories that were part of every civilization's culture. The invention of the camera only helped cement the notion that ghosts really did exist. Humans had actually photographed Huelowens' standing at the windows in abandoned houses, and these photos would appear in publications for the entire world to see. The door opened and Roy stepped through the threshold, and into the Doctor's office, he spoke to Ben, "Robert has started painting, and although he has not started to remember past lives through his dreams, I do think that he may reach that point." "What kinds of paintings are we talking about," asked Ben. Mostly landscapes drawn from memory, but he has drawn something else from memory, and she is stunning," said Roy. "You can only be referring to one woman," said a not too surprised Ben. "You knew?" asked a dumbfounded Roy. "We haven't had anyone paint a portrait of her in over five hundred years, and I do know that he has a deep feeling for her, and she has similar feelings towards him" stated Ben as he continued, "no human could ever resist the lure of Aphrodite, the goddess of love." "I have enlisted the services of Edward Chow to help with the paintings, and I am going to suggest to Robert that he should enroll in some class study, at least that way we can monitor his work," said Roy. "Well done Roy, you and I can get updates from Edward, we are still in control of the situation, and I will send for Cassandra, to see if she has had any contact with previous versions of Robert Marshall." Roy stood and saluted the head council member, he stepped through the closet door and was gone. The council could communicate to one another through mental telepathy. They were more advanced mentally than their human descendants because they had the time to be so. If a man could live a thousand lifetimes he too would seem god-like to the rest of the population, it was just that simple. Ben had spoken telepathically to Cassandra, and as he opened the closet door she stepped inside. Time had been kind to the woman the ancient Greeks knew as Aphrodite, and the modern world knew as Cassandra. She sat gracefully in a chair across from Ben's desk. He needed to ask her some questions about Robert Marshall. "I know you better than anybody on the planet, so please tell me the truth about your connection with Robert Marshall," asked Ben. Cassandra spoke softly to Ben, "I did have a romantic connection to a soldier in the civil war, he died in 1863, and I can sense a piece of that soldier in Robert Marshall, but that's all. Remember you asked me to show myself to him in your waiting room, we had to know if he would turn into a floater, but that hasn't happened, has it?" asked Cassandra. "I think you should see the painting this man did of you, it is in Edward Chow's studio," said Ben. "Look at that painting and tell me yourself if you think we have anything to worry about." Cassandra agreed to visit Edward Chow. She stood and gave Ben Biggles the customary acknowledgement that was required. Her next stop would be to the Chow studio. She only visited him when a human had painted a portrait of her. It seemed not so long ago that she was asked to look at a painting of herself, she knew this was not the case, for the Leonardo painting was showing the telltale signs of age. The new painting by Robert Marshall had many similarities, only to Cassandra it seemed to capture her in a way that was beyond description. He had managed to capture her real eye colours, could that have been from that very brief encounter at Ben Biggles office? She knew the answer, but didn't tell Edward. She was at the civil war battle without her contact lens when she looked into the eyes of the dying Everett Gentry, it was the last image he saw before moving on to a new life, and now, all of these years later, she was certain that Robert had painted her from that encounter, and he had been Everett Gentry in a previous life. She had a propensity for loving human men, and over time that love became legendary. Time has a strange way of distorting the truth, and only one member of the council knew that Aphrodite really only had one human lover through the years. He understood and left her alone, and never admitted to her that he knew. He would no longer be able to eliminate Robert Marshall, he would have to explain it to the others only if it became absolutely necessary. She had developed the ability to locate that one special human through their dreams, but not all of her conquests were able to remember her. Robert had the dreams only for a brief time, but they were enough for Cassandra to latch onto, and now she was excited to rekindle the romance with Robert Marshall. This new painting showed that he really did remember her from a previous life, and she would again show herself to him. She needed to plan it carefully, she knew that she only needed to appear before him briefly. She had to make it appear to the council that she was unaware of his presence. She knew where she would meet him, she had been secretly watching him having lunch at a small but busy café near his work. Ben had sent Roy to the ruins in Pompeii, and at that moment she realized for certain that Ben really did know what she was going to do, and in his own way gave her his blessing.

Robert was at work, and Roy Summerset was nowhere to be seen. He sent a text to Roy but there was no response. "That's just great, sitting alone at lunch," Robert thought to himself. He had no way of knowing that the ancient gods were at work in modern America. He almost didn't go to the café for lunch, but he was a creature of habit, and he didn't like change. He sat down alone at a small table for two. He had ordered a sandwich and bowl of soup, and didn't even want to look up for fear of having to talk with anyone else, but for some reason he felt a presence in the café. He looked up and saw a woman, she was facing away from him, but her beautiful long black hair caught his attention. He stared at this woman, and as she turned with coffee in hand, she smiled at him. Was it her? He was not quite certain of that, her eyes were not different colours, they were both a brilliant green and for a moment he just stared. She walked towards the door, and Robert stood quickly, too quickly. Soup spilled over the leg of his pants. "Shit," was all Robert said. He had looked down at the mess, and tried wiping it with his napkin. The person at the next table saw the state Robert was in and handed him his napkins. Robert looked up from the mess and saw his mystery girl walking away down the street. Robert ran past several people, and they were yelling at him. He got out the door and looked down the street, she couldn't have gone far, but Robert could not see her. He ran in the same direction, but it would be of no use. She had gone up a side street and vanished, and all Robert could do was make his way back to the office. He didn't even have Roy to talk with about the latest sighting of this mystery woman. Roy did send him a text later in the afternoon telling Robert he thought he might have food poisoning and he was going to be home for several days. Robert read the message and sent back a brief note telling Roy he hoped he felt better soon. He didn't even mention seeing the woman to Roy again, he didn't think his sick friend would want to hear anything about it. Roy read the brief note, but he had other things to attend to. Scientists were very close to a chamber in Pompeii that contained some Huelowen artifacts. Many Huelowens were lost in that terrible natural disaster, they had moved to the base of Mt. Vesuvius to be away from human contact, and in doing so sealed their fate. Now all these years later, humans were excavating that Huelowen grave site. Roy had visited Pompeii when it was a thriving concern, and he was one of the last council members to visit before the catastrophe, he told fellow Huelowens to flee, most did, but to the ones who had been instructed to remain in the chamber under the city and guard the secrets of Huelowen civilization there would be no rescue. The area and structures had been covered with a thick layer of dust, and when humans found well preserved buildings and bodies, the council began to worry. What if they located the entrance to the hidden world of the Huelowen? The council could not risk the discovery, and when Ben received word that humans were getting close to finding the entrance, he sent the last council member who had visited the chamber. Roy remembered the inside of these rooms well, he would need to if he was going to teleport into the chambers. The first trip inside the chamber went exactly as planned, and on his return trip he enlisted the help of several Huelowen. They all held hands, and Roy transported them inside the chambers again. It would require several days to remove the artifacts and bodies from this chamber and transport them to a safe location. Roy had successfully completed his mission, the archaeologists would very shortly discover this empty hidden chamber, and nothing in man's future would be altered.

Chapter 5

Robert decided that after work he would drop by the Edward Chow art studio and check on the status of his paintings. That was the excuse he had come up with to visit the studio. He really just wanted to look at the painting he had done of the black haired woman, and compare her to the woman he had seen at the café. He walked past the studio, and noticed a sign on the front door that read, Sorry for the inconvenience, will reopen next week. He proceeded home to his apartment, and decided that if he could not see the painting, he would create another. He started to paint, again from memory, only this time the image was even more striking than it had been previously. The next few days at work passed quickly, and each night was filled with the painting of a goddess. He gave her the green matching eyes he had seen at the café, and later that night after he shut off the lights, the strange dreams he had experienced in the hospital returned.

His name was Ganda, and he found himself chained in the belly of a slave ship, headed for South Carolina. The smells and conditions on the ship were inhumane, he had no idea of the time it had taken to cross from Africa to the port that they were to be unloaded. He was happy to have at least survived the crossing, he had no idea what was in store for him once he was onshore. Many had perished during the trip, and their bodies were taken topside. Ganda could hear the splashes, and was certain that if he died he too would be cast over the side. He was cleaned and put on a stage, his chains had been removed and as he looked out onto the crowd he understood what was happening. He had been sold to a plantation owner, who claimed Ganda as his own, and renamed him John. He was placed in shackles and transported away by wagon. He didn't know what was in store for him at the plantation, but soon enough he would find out how evil some men could be. He had never experienced this kind of pain before, he was whipped when he didn't do as he was told. He was not to use his African name, and must remember that his new name was John. He received the absolute minimum in both food and clothing, he slept in a small building with ten others, and after a few years of the abuse he thought of nothing else but escape. He was told one day that he had been sold to a new master, and that was when his life changed. He was struck repeatedly on the head by his first owners foreman, and shortly afterwards he began to have strange dreams. They were beyond his understanding, but one of the things in his dreams was not. A beautiful black haired woman. He saw her night after night in dreams that made no sense to him. One day he was transported to a new home, and while working in the field he saw her. She was a beautiful young woman with long black hair, and the greenest eyes Ganda had ever seen. He was certain that he had seen her before, in a dream perhaps, he wasn't really sure, and as he stared at her he was strapped by the field foreman. He was not allowed to look directly at her, and he was going to pay the price. The woman stopped the foreman, and spoke to Ganda. He was not supposed to look at her directly, but he did. She smiled at him, and he knew at that moment that they had met before. Ganda believed that people lived previous lives, and he knew in his heart and soul that she was a part of that life. He didn't know who she was and didn't care. She looked at him and he could feel her love, he couldn't explain it. She told him her name was Cassandra, and that she was going to be staying on at the plantation visiting her uncle. She had the foreman show her where Ganda lived, it was a small tarpaper shack, and she only needed to see the inside once. He was asleep that night when he started to dream of someone curled up against him. He awoke from the dream and found that he had his arms around Cassandra, how she got here was a mystery to Ganda, but he didn't care. He knew that if anyone saw what was going on in that shack he would be put to death. The colour of her skin would demand that. He had been with this woman before, but he knew that this was impossible, at least in this lifetime. How she arrived unnoticed to him in that shack was a total mystery until the night he stayed awake, watching. Ganda was scared out of his wits, as he saw her materialize in front of him. In his mind she was some kind of spirit, he jumped from his blanket, burst through the door and fled the shack screaming. He heard the shots, and then he felt a stinging in his back. He fell to the ground and as his eyes closed he heard the bells ringing.

Robert slammed his hand down on the alarm clock, and as he lay in bed he began to wonder if he was seeing a previous life, was it someone else's life or his own. He couldn't be sure, but he did remember a few things, and per his doctors instructions he was to write down everything that he could remember. The memory was fleeting, so he wrote quickly. He was from Africa, and sold into slavery, his name was Ganda, and he was involved with a white woman. He wrote down her name, Cassandra. Robert stopped writing, he knew that this could never have happened. It was just a crazy dream, it had to be. He remembered the woman in the dream and knew she was the same one from the café. He got out of bed and walked directly towards the painting in the living room, but he stood in disbelief, as the painting he had finished the night before was gone, in its place on the easel sat a blank canvas. Robert could not believe his eyes. He had painted her, he was certain of that, but he wasn't certain of anything, not anymore. The painting was gone, and as he checked the door and windows he realised that no one had entered his apartment and taken it. Why would anyone take my painting? Robert thought to himself. Nobody even knew he painted, and then he stopped. Roy and Edward Chow were the only two people who had seen his work, and been in his apartment. Roy was sick, and Mr. Chow was out of town, still, Robert's mind wouldn't stop thinking about the possibilities. How did they get in, neither man had a key, and nothing was unlocked. He then wondered if he was having a relapse, did he just imagine that he had painted a second portrait, which was much more plausible. The thought of either Roy or Edward being in his apartment made Robert laugh. Why would either man take a painting of a woman neither man said they knew? Almost all humans had the same weakness, and the Huelowen's had been taking advantage of that since their creation on this planet. Their minds would not accept the obvious, and would find the path of least resistance. This always led them away from discovering the truth on Earth.

Robert was right about someone entering his apartment, and taking his painting, but his mind was moving the same way as water running in a stream. It was taking the path of least resistance, and leading him away from the truth.

Roy Summerset and Edward Chow had returned from their adventure in Italy. Roy knew something strange had happened to Robert while he was away. He didn't know exactly what it was but he believed it had to do with Cassandra. He materialized that night in Robert's apartment, and when he saw the new painting of Cassandra, with her matching green eyes he knew that she had again shown herself to Robert. He grabbed the painting from the easel and vanished, he would return later with a blank canvas in an attempt to confuse Robert. He knew that when Robert looked at the blank canvas he would not be able to comprehend what had happened. Roy contacted Ben Biggles, and materialized in his closet a few moments later. He wanted Ben to see the painting, but he also wanted to know what was really going on. Roy held the painting up for Ben to see, and then said, "What the hell is going on here? I thought you told Cassandra to keep away from this human, but I now know that you are aware of something else." Ben asked Roy to sit down and he would try to explain. "This man is special to Cassandra, she has been in love with his essence since near the beginning of our breeding program on this planet. She has not loved hundreds of men as we were led to believe, but just one, and Robert is now that one. She has been able to find them when they dream of a previous life with her." "We have been removing these floaters from the program, and now you tell me that this floater is different," said Roy as he continued, "I am going to insist on a council meeting. We must confront Cassandra on this issue, and then the council can vote on the direction we should take in this matter." Roy stood and with painting in hand said, "I will take this with me to the meeting for the others to see." He gave Ben the obligatory hand gesture, and then he passed through the closet door and was gone. Ben summoned Cassandra mentally to his office, and when she appeared he told her that Roy was going to tell the council about her manipulation of Robert. Ben held out little hope that they could persuade the others that Robert didn't pose a real threat to life on earth. Sure, others had told stories of previous lives, but the general population ridiculed that person without any influence from the Huelowen council. This was going to be different, and all Cassandra could do was wait to be heard at the council meeting.

The meeting was held on a weekend, it was the only time that the twelve council members could convene without drawing attention to themselves. They no longer met on Mt. Olympus, this site had been compromised years earlier, and once evidence of the Huelowen council was removed, that site was only remembered and passed on through stories told over the centuries, and now what was once fact became legend. The new site was away from prying eyes, it was directly under the ancient Mayan ruins, and was now only accessible by teleportation. The council members arrived and Ben took his rightful place in the center seat. He had many names through the years, but his face had changed little. When they were on Mt. Olympus he was known as Zeus, but he hadn't used that name in a very long time, and as he looked at the others he wasn't sure what they would say to Aphrodite. She too had used many names over the years, but had settled on Cassandra for the last few hundred years. Roy arrived and then, as the meeting was to start, Cassandra materialized and sat alone in a chair facing the other members. Roy started to present his evidence against Robert Marshall, a human, and walked over and uncovered the painting of Cassandra. "I present to you a painting of the great Aphrodite, the human who painted this portrait will very shortly become a floater. He is already dreaming of her, he has told me this himself, this is his second painting of her in as many weeks, only this painting was obviously done from one of those past lives, since she was instructed not to see him again. We have all agreed to keep a low profile and not expose the humans to our existence on this planet. We therefore have no choice but to send this human over to the other side. If we restart him, he will not discover what we have tried so long to conceal." Ben could not let this continue, for if he did he knew that Cassandra, as she was now calling herself, would lose a man she had loved for most of her time on earth. "Hear me first," said Ben, "I have not been truthful to my brothers and sisters on this council, especially you Roy, I have known for some time that Cassandra has loved the same being's essence for thousands of years. She did in fact show herself to Robert Marshall last week, and he painted her from that meeting. I am acting as his Doctor, and he has yet to tell me of any dreams he has had since his accident. He poses no danger to us at this time or to himself. He had not even told Roy of any new dreams." Several of the council members questioned Roy, and when it became obvious that this human had not had any dreams since his accident they turned their attention towards Cassandra. She was careful of what she said, "I know you believe I have had my way with many humans, but I have actually been faithful to just one human over the centuries. I am only able to locate the soul when it calls to me in a dream. I have had encounters with that essence when it returns both as man or woman. I also have come to realise something else that the council is not aware of. Humans find their mates in life using the same process. We all know that these humans are returning over and over in many forms, if the council decides to restart Robert Marshall, that entity will also be drawn to me. It is fate or destiny, you can call it what you will, but we will always find each other. This time however, I sense something different, and I would like the blessing of the council to see it through." The council started to talk amongst themselves and after only a short deliberation voted on the life of Robert Marshall. They were always a compassionate group, and today voted to allow Cassandra to continue with developing a relationship with Robert Marshall. Ben would continue to monitor the situation as Robert's Doctor, and Roy would continue watching as Robert's best friend. The new painting of Cassandra had been sent to the vault at Edward Chow's studio to join the others. Robert was not aware of what had transpired that weekend, or to how close he was to becoming reset.

Robert and Roy continued their friendship, and Robert was happy to have him back at work. Roy continued to press Robert about dreams and about his mystery woman. It was when Roy asked Robert if he had done any new paintings and Robert grew suspicious. Roy was acting differently towards Robert, and Robert could feel the tension between them. Robert soon realized that all Roy was asking about with any consistency was dreams and paintings. Robert wisely choose to no longer confide in his friend. He decided on a visit with Edward Chow after work, he wanted to retrieve the painting he had done of Cassandra. He was upset upon arriving there to learn that the painting had been sold, and that his other works were still available. "Why would someone want a portrait of a stranger hanging on their wall?" asked Robert. Edward had an answer and although it was one he hadn't used in five hundred years, it still applied to the situation today. A man entered the gallery, took one look at your painting, and started to cry. He said it looked very similar to his now deceased wife, and he just couldn't leave without purchasing it. Robert wondered if this was the woman he had seen. He didn't ask Edward any more questions, he left the studio disappointed and proceeded home. That night, as he slept, he again dreamed of strange and yet familiar surroundings.

His name was Everett and he was a young man from Ohio who lived on a farm with his parents. He remembered joining the union army, and the last night that he spent with his girl. Her name was Cassandra, she had long black hair and the greenest eyes Everett had ever seen. He loved her, and told her that he used to have strange dreams, and that she was in those dreams. She smiled at Everett, and told him that she felt the same way. They cuddled and kissed until Everett's father called for him, he was leaving tomorrow and would not see her again until after the war. It was not going to end well for Everett, and as he lay dying on the battlefield, he again saw Cassandra, but something was different about her eyes. She was kneeling over him and told him they would meet again. The alarm clock woke Robert, and as he wrote about this life, he realized that the dreams were occurring more frequently. He had some crazy dreams in the hospital, but that was almost a year earlier. He did not dream about being someone else every night, but the frequency over the last month had increased. He had not told anyone of these dreams, but one person was able to sense them, Cassandra.

Roy was once again missing work, only this time it was to give Cassandra room to meet Robert. She had planned to meet him at the small café, he again sat alone at a small table for two, and was shocked when Cassandra asked if she could join him. Fortunately for Robert he had already finished a bowl of soup, when she approached. "Hello, may

I join you for lunch, Robert" asked Cassandra. Robert could not believe his eyes or ears. He had never met her before, but she knew his name, and he in turn believed he knew hers. It was the black haired beauty he had not only seen, but dreamed of over the last year. He couldn't speak initially, but soon found himself blithering his life story to her. He knew nothing about her, but was pleasantly surprised to find that, as he spoke, he really did believe he had known this woman his entire life. She introduced herself as Cassandra, and without saying another word she placed her hand on his. He knew who she was, and in that instant he realised that his dreams were really past lives. He was one of the lucky few who had been allowed a glimpse into the past, his own past. He had been many people, he wasn't really sure how many, but he did know that this woman was in every dream he had experienced so far. He had loved her before, and knew he would always love her. It was a strange feeling, she had mismatched eyes, and he wondered if she had worn contact lens the last time he had seen her. "I know what you're thinking, yes I wear contact lens to hide my abnormality," said Cassandra. Robert was hoping to spend more time with Cassandra, but she abruptly stood up and told him she would meet him again tomorrow. He watched as she left the café, but he couldn't be certain if he had just imagined the entire meeting. He went back to work, but couldn't stop thinking about Cassandra. Would he really see her again tomorrow? He arrived home to his apartment and after dinner sat watching the television. He couldn't control his dreams, or when he would have them, and as he drifted off to sleep he was thinking of her. However, the dream he would have tonight would not be with her.

The weather was warm and the wind was blowing gently across a field of wheat. Rebecca was watching from the kitchen window as a small army of men were cutting the wheat with scythes and standing it for collection. The door opened and her husband entered the room. "Do you have the meal ready for the men, they will be in shortly?" "Yes dear we are ready," Rebecca answered. She looked at her children who were helping with every aspect of the harvest. She had bore nine children for her husband. Five boys to work the fields and four daughters to help with housework. Farming was difficult work, but with the children grown and helping out, it was not quite as difficult as it had been when they were first married. Rebecca had little trouble giving birth, and as the number of children grew so did her ability to recover from the one that came before. They had arrived by covered wagon, and set out to settle in the area. They had built a barn to house the animals first. It would have seemed silly to an outsider that you would protect your animals first, but if you didn't protect them, you would most likely not make it through the first winter on the plains. Rebecca smiled to herself as she watched her daughter's buzzing around the kitchen. They were learning from their mother, all of the things they would need to be able to survive on a farm with their men when the time arose.

The first child was born in that barn with their first calf, and now all of these years later they had built a house large enough for the entire family. The kitchen was the largest room in the house, and the table was hand built and large enough for all the men who worked in the field to sit around. Rebecca and her daughters would be responsible to feed them at dinner and supper time. She stepped outside the house to watch the action in the distance. Two of her sons were gathering the wheat bundles and placing them on a horse drawn wagon. The wagon then made the trek to the stationary threshing machine, a large steam traction engine was connected by a long belt to the thresher, and her son Henry, named after her husband, was helping one of the men who was part of the crew to feed the wheat into the machine. She marvelled at how things had changed on the farm since the arrival of this large machinery. Her husband could grow more wheat now than would have ever been possible when they first arrived here thirty years earlier. The whistle blew on the large steam powered machine signalling the break for dinner. The men made their way to the farmhouse, and after washing off the dust from the crop, they sat at the large kitchen table. The women had prepared large quantities of food, and as the men ate they talked about how good the wheat crop was. The man who owned the farm machinery travelled the country side and he would compare what he saw coming out of the thresher with the neighbouring farmer's crops. He was the person that Henry listened to as he spoke. This man told Henry that his wheat was the best he had seen so far, and Henry knew that meant that this year his farm would make some money, and as he ate he felt the anxiety slip away from him. The last weeks before wheat harvest were always the most stressful for him. If the rains came at the wrong time the crop would suffer, not enough rain and the crop would be ruined. The last week before harvest saw perfect weather conditions. No rain and little humidity meant Henry and his wife would have a successful year on the farm. "Nothing could go wrong now," said Henry. The entire table fell silent at the remark, and Henry realized that he may have jinxed the harvest, quickly he knocked on the table, and the rest of the men started talking again. That afternoon work continued and as suppertime approached the sound of the steam whistle surprised Rebecca. It wasn't yet time to stop, and then her heart sank, the whistle was blowing two long and one short, and it repeated again, two long and one short. Rebecca and her husband and the entire team were told by the steam traction owner that if an accident were to occur he would alert everyone in earshot of a problem using the steam whistle. Rebecca stood in the doorway, she could not move, her mind was comprehending the sounds coming from the field in the distance. She heard it again, and this time she ran to the field, her daughters running behind her, and as she got closer, her husband Henry stopped her. "Don't go any further Rebecca, it's our boy Henry, he slipped off the top of the thresher and his legs are caught in the drum. The drum was just that, a circular drum that turned at five hundred revolutions per minute. The wheat was fed by hand into the top of the thresher and as it passed by the drum the kernels of wheat were separated from the stalk. Henry's legs were now crushed by that drum, and Rebecca ran past her husband to see her son. He was still alive and told his mother not to worry that he would be alright, but she knew that was untrue. It was a slow agonizing death, and waiting for the doctor only made things worse. The young man now was groaning in pain, and the strain on

Rebecca was just too great. She dropped to the ground with a pain in her chest, her arm was numb, and as her husband Henry held her she heard the ringing of bells. "Do you hear that Henry?" Rebecca said through the pain. Robert slammed his hand down on the alarm clock. Sweat ran down his face, his heart was pounding, it had seemed so real to him as he lay in bed wondering what he had just experienced, and was it real or not.

He had a pad of paper ready beside the bed and he quickly wrote everything he could remember from this latest dream. The memory was fading, but he did write down some astonishing facts. He was a woman in this dream, she had a husband, with nine children. They were farmers, and her son was crushed in some sort of farm machinery. Robert remembered that in this dream he was called Rebecca, and that she collapsed and died beside the machine. Robert thought about what he had written, and he now couldn't remember anything else. He jumped in the shower and as the warm water ran over his face and down his body he began thinking about his dreams. He had now experienced life as both man and woman. He wondered if everyone had these memories locked away inside them, and did his head injury somehow allow him to access these previous lives. Could it really be that simple? He was drying himself off, and reading the hastily written notes. It appeared as though they were in chronological order. He had only experienced these dreams sporadically since the accident, but each one since that time seemed to be at a later date. He somehow believed that Cassandra held the answers he was searching for, and when they met for lunch he would ask her. He was wondering if Roy was OK, as this was the second day that he was not at work. His only thought was that he was actually happy that Roy was away, he didn't need Roy barging in on their private time. He was going to tell Cassandra exactly what he thought was happening, and he hoped that she didn't think he needed to see a shrink. The morning passed quickly, and soon Robert found himself seated across from Cassandra. After exchanging pleasantries Robert came directly to the point. "I have been having some very odd dreams, and some of those dreams include you, only none of the people you are with appear to be me." Robert stopped, "well what I mean to say is, I know it's me but I am in someone else's body, does that make any sense to you?" Cassandra looked around the café before speaking, "I do know what is happening to you, and no, you are not crazy, but we can't talk about it here, can I meet with you tonight at your place?" Robert was excited and obviously it showed on his face. "We will just be talking, OK?" said Cassandra. Robert was certain that his face was bright red. He was embarrassed, but regained his composure, and after giving his address to her she stood, said goodbye, and was gone. Robert was left wondering what she could possibly want to tell him in private that she couldn't reveal at the café. He returned to work, but the anticipation of having this beauty at his apartment made it seem as though the afternoon was moving along at a crawl. Robert got off work and raced home, he had to eat, and then whip his apartment into shape. The bell rang at seven thirty, and Robert opened the door and invited Cassandra in. She had never been in his apartment, but now as she looked around she could picture it in her mind, and could materialize here at any time. Robert offered her a drink, and she sat in a single recliner directly opposite from the couch. Robert sat on the couch and waited for her to speak. "I said you weren't crazy, and that I could explain," said Cassandra, "but first you have to promise me that you won't tell anyone. What I tell you tonight will leave you with even more questions, and we can meet here at your place until you fully understand." Robert promised that he could keep quiet and that he would not tell anybody anything that he and Cassandra spoke about. "If you do tell anyone, I will not be able to protect you, do you understand," asked

Cassandra. Robert was wondering what the hell he was getting himself into, but he agreed.

Cassandra began slowly and carefully, if she didn't he would think that she was even crazier than he was. She asked Robert if he could explain to her what he really thought was occurring. "I have been writing down what I remember when I awaken," said Robert. "That's a good start, now tell me what you think is happening to you?" said Cassandra. Robert told her that he believed that he was seeing previous lives, he wasn't sure who these people were, but he thought that they might be him. "One thing makes me realize that these are just dreams and not previous life experiences," explained Robert as he continued, "you are in some of my dreams, and that is not possible." Cassandra asked Robert to grab the notes he had written, and when he returned she asked him to tell her a small portion of each dream. Robert started reading the first story when Cassandra stopped him. "Yes, I do remember meeting you, it was in a field, and you were an African slave, your name was Ganda, but they called you John," stated Cassandra. Robert had shivers running down his back, and he stared at her in total disbelief. "How the hell could you know that, I haven't told a soul," said Robert. Cassandra continued, "You were a young man from Ohio, and you joined the union army to fight against slavery.

Your name was Everett Gentry, and I was your girl." Robert stood up, "This must be some kind of trick, you couldn't possibly have been there. Who are you?" Cassandra smiled at Robert and asked him to sit down. "The last dream you were a woman, your name was Rebecca, you don't remember me from that life because I never get involved with humans that have already selected a mate." Robert was dumbfounded, he was freaking out. "You have my apartment bugged, and it was you who took my painting, and read my notes. Yes, that would make sense, that has to be what happened," explained Robert. Cassandra knew humans had real trouble believing, they had to see things with their own eyes and she thought of a way to end this once and for all. "Please Robert take my hand, and I will show you something that will help you understand." Robert was frightened, he didn't know if he should take her hand, maybe she was from a secret government agency, and she would twist his arm around and …., he had been watching too much television, but eventually reached his hand out to her. She smiled again at him and told him, "Do not under any circumstance let go of my hand." Robert wasn't sure of what was happening, he felt strange, but only for a few seconds. The two were no longer in Robert's apartment, and it took some time for his eyes to focus, he was still holding

Cassandra's hand. "You will be alright, just give it some time. Robert's head was throbbing, but soon the feeling had passed and he found himself standing in a room lined with paintings. He had no idea what had happened to him, but he soon noticed the paintings were all of the same person, Cassandra. Robert just stood in amazement, he was gazing at the works of art. He wouldn't have believed it if he hadn't seen it with his own eyes, and even then he was having trouble comprehending the situation. Cassandra had told him not to touch anything, and he complied. He came across both of his paintings and knew that she had been in his apartment and stolen his last painting, and that she must have purchased the other from Mr. Chow. He wasn't sure what had happened or how he got here, he thought that maybe she had drugged him, and wondered why she would have all these paintings of herself. He felt the hair stand on the back of his neck as he looked closely at the other paintings in the room. He was standing in front of a painting that was similar to his only this one was signed by Leonardo da Vinci. He looked closely at her face, it was Cassandra, but how could that be? He was convinced that this was some sort of trick, it had to be, and if it wasn't, Robert took a step back from Cassandra. 'Do you expect me to believe that you are some kind of witch?" asked Robert. "I am not a witch, although over the years, people did believe we were witches some of us were even burned. Humans have always felt that they needed to destroy what they didn't understand," finished Cassandra. "Humans, you said humans," he took two more steps back from her before continuing, I don't understand why are you telling me this." He placed his hands over his face, and he felt her hand over his, then he felt strange again. He was dizzy now and Cassandra helped him sit down on his couch. He was back in his own apartment, he had no idea if he was dreaming or tripping on some strange drug. Cassandra was sitting down beside him now, she was still holding his hand. "Are you OK?" she asked. Robert wasn't sure what the hell he was, he wasn't sure of anything. Cassandra had grabbed a beer out of Robert's refrigerator, and after opening it, handed it to him. He thanked her and proceeded to drink it, and when he was finished he looked carefully at her. He had settled down now, and finally just asked her what she meant when she said humans. Cassandra looked at Robert and told him that he had enough excitement for one night, and they could continue again tomorrow night. She reminded him of their agreement, and walked to the door. Robert asked her one more question before she left. "I have read about people teleporting, and is that what happened to me tonight?" Cassandra interceded, "I think you have seen enough for one night, don't you?" She opened the door and kissed Robert goodnight on the cheek. He closed the door and sat quietly on the couch, and after a few moments he felt sleepy. He was barely able to make it to the bedroom before succumbing to the drug placed in his beer by Cassandra. He slept soundly, and in the morning awoke to a pleasant dream about the woman that he had spent the previous evening with. He showered and proceeded to work, as though nothing had happened. Roy was at work today, and although Robert wanted to tell him about Cassandra he had promised her that he would not tell a soul. Roy was more nosey than usual, asking more questions. Had he any new dreams? Or visions about the mystery woman? Robert told him he had not seen her, and he hadn't had any strange dreams. He wasn't sure if Roy believed him, but he left Robert alone for the rest of the day.

Robert waited patiently for that evening, and was surprised when there was a knock on his door. He opened the door and Cassandra entered, she sat on the couch and had Robert sit beside her. "I was thinking that you might just materialize in my apartment tonight," Robert said with anticipation. "I didn't want to frighten you this evening," she said with a smile on her face. Robert was actually happy that she did not, but he was wondering what strange things she would tell him tonight. "Do you have any questions you would like to ask before I begin?" asked Cassandra. Robert didn't know what he should ask her when it just came out of his mouth. "Who are you?" Cassandra smiled at Robert before she spoke. "I'm not sure if you are ready, after all I have not confided in any human, you would be the first. Robert picked up on what she said and immediately spoke, "You said something about humans last night, don't tell me that you are not human." Cassandra smiled, "Ok, I won't tell you that I'm not human." Robert was wondering what institution she had escaped from when he asked her, "if you are not human, then tell me what are you?" Cassandra was waiting for the appropriate time, and it was now or never, "I told you before if I continue tonight, there's no going back, do you understand? Robert saw the look on her face as she told him, and he knew she was serious. "Yes, please continue," said Robert. "I am Huelowen, and I came from a distant dying planet that we called earth." Robert started laughing, "Did Roy put you up to this?" he asked. Cassandra stopped, she seemed to be concentrating on something. Robert sat in total silence as his friend Roy materialized directly in front of him. "Hello, Robert." The scream was unexpected, and it even surprised Cassandra. "You sound like a little girl," Roy said. "What the hell, who are you people?" Robert again asked. "I told you this wouldn't work, but at least he didn't tell me about you today at lunch," said Roy. "Are you both …," Robert didn't get the chance to finish his sentence. "Huelowen, yes we are," said Cassandra, and she thanked Roy for his help. Roy looked at Robert and before he vanished said, "Not one word, OK pal!" Robert nodded and Roy was gone. "Can I continue now?" said Cassandra. Robert didn't answer and she accepted his silence as confirmation to continue, "We came to this planet more than five thousand years ago. We procreated with the most advanced indigenous bipeds on your planet, and humans were the resulting offspring." Robert stared at her in amazement, he believed that there were others outside of this world, but now that he was confronted with the truth he still wasn't sure. Cassandra saw the look on Robert's face and said, "You still don't believe me." "I am finding it very difficult to believe that you are a five thousand year old alien, you look like a thirty - five year old Italian, and Roy looks like a forty year old American Indian," said Robert. Cassandra decided it best to start at the very beginning and give Robert a history lesson, one that he didn't learn at school.

"Our scientists were working on gene modification in order to prolong our lives, and allow us to travel further into space. It was purely by accident that this modification resulted in our bodies being able to regenerate, giving us a life as close to immortality as possible. We will eventually die, and because of one rogue scientist who poisoned the water, and killed so many of us on our home planet, we had no choice but to leave and travel to this planet. We, over time, slowly integrated and bred with the people living here, creating a new species, Humans. We found out that children born to pure Huelowen had the same virtual immortality as their parents, but that as blood lines were diluted so was life expectancy. The Huelowen council of twelve, moved to the top of Mt. Olympus, and from that location became the overseers of the humans. Most of the Huelowen population that had been spread across the continents gathered and formed the city of Atlantis, they were lost when it sank into the sea." Robert was completely shocked by this incredible story, but something deep inside his mind told him that the story was true, and that he should just listen. "I'll get you a beer," she said as she stood up, she returned with an open beer, and as he drank she told him that he had again heard enough for one night. "Don't worry, she said, "we can continue tomorrow," she leaned over and kissed him on the lips, and after saying good night she vanished.

Robert was no longer surprised, and he couldn't believe how quickly he was accepting her at her word. He again started to believe it was just a dream, and that he would wake from it at any time. He finished the beer, and immediately felt groggy, he again just made it to his bed before the drug she had placed in his beer took effect. He awoke in the morning not realizing that Cassandra had been slipping him a mickey each night, and went to work each day as though nothing was different. He was hoping that the day would pass quickly, he wondered as he walked to work if he would see Roy, and if he really was a Huelowen, why was he working at the call center? He walked in and saw Roy, who smiled and waved. "Well that's not weird," Robert thought to himself. The day passed and the two met for lunch, they talked about everything and nothing, and Robert began wondering if Roy was part of last night's festivities or if he had imagined it. Roy shattered that thought when he said to Robert on the way out for the day, "Have fun tonight." Robert smiled sheepishly, all he could muster was, "Thanks." Robert arrived home and decided to surf the internet before Cassandra arrived. He knew the legend behind the Greek gods living on Mt. Olympus, but as he did he wondered if Cassandra was on Mt. Olympus. Could she be one of the twelve that made up this

Huelowen council? He knew that all legends are based loosely on factual events, and the legends refer to twelve gods and goddesses. He also found that they referred to seven males and five females. Could he actually be meeting with a goddess, and if he was, which one was she? He initially had removed Aphrodite as she was described by many as blonde, with different eye colours, and Robert was ready to move on when he read that her hair colour could be different to different individuals. She had shown him a room with paintings hanging from the walls. They all portrayed her with long black hair, and he had painted her with different coloured eyes. Could she really be Aphrodite, and was this how he envisioned her, and if so, were all the paintings in that room works that he in his previous lives had done? She was the most beautiful creature he had ever seen, and when he heard something in the living room he hoped it was her. She was sitting on his couch, and he without fear walked over and sat down beside her. "Are you ready for the next instalment?" asked Cassandra. Robert nodded, he was having trouble speaking to her since believing she was in fact Aphrodite, the goddess of love.

Cassandra started where she had left off the night before, "The council was increased to fourteen members when we left our home planet but two were lost on the way to this planet. The twelve of us moved to Mt. Olympus, and over time the population called us gods. We were not gods, but our arrogance led to unrest and when the council found out of a plan by the Mayan civilization to expose themselves as Huelowen to the rest of the world, we did an unspeakable thing. The council agreed to use the same poisonous compound used on our home planet to destroy them. In the end all that remained were the buildings, we removed any evidence in that city and placed it in what would eventually become the new meeting place of the council. It is directly under the Mayan ruins, and acts as a constant reminder to the evil we committed so long ago. You asked me yesterday to explain our skin colour to you, and I didn't respond. The first astronauts visiting your planet returned with news of advanced civilizations here, and over the years more ships were sent to gather information. When we discovered that our planet was dying we sent ships again only this time their mission was to gather specimens from each advanced civilization. We realized upon examination that we were not that different, we thought that the inhabitants of your planet, known to us as Man, may have been placed on that world by a distant relative of our own. It was at this time that a scientist working with one of those specimens found out by accident that the gene modification enabled us to not only change skin colour, but also to change form. That scientist touched one of his patients without wearing gloves and immediately changed from our grey skin to brown, and before you say anything, remember that on this planet there are many creatures that can do the same, the chameleon is a perfect example. This allowed us to blend in and take the form of all races on this planet." Robert was now beginning to understand, and the story was taking on a new meaning. This creature from another world, was giving him a crash course in Huelowen history on this planet. She told Robert that they went to great lengths to hide their existence here, so why was she telling him? "I don't understand why you have confided in me," Robert asked, "What makes me so special?" "In your dreams of past lives we were lovers, and I thought you would have realized that I have been following you through time," Cassandra continued, "I can't find you with every new life that you experience, but if for some reason you dream of our past life together, your dreams are like homing beacons for me to follow. You hit your head in that car accident and when you were in the hospital you dreamed of a life with me, we arrived here to make certain that once you recovered that you no longer had these dreams. We found out that humans who have continued these dreams eventually realize that they are dreaming of previous lives, and some of them, we call them floaters, will actually remember things that could compromise us." "Do you kill those people who float?" asked Robert. "Yes, but you must realize that no human ever dies, they are reborn into a new life," said Cassandra. "Am I to be reborn?" asked Robert. "Not yet, I told the council that I have loved you, in your many different forms since the program started, and I believe that something great is in store for you, and me," stated Cassandra. "I now have even more questions than answers," said Robert. Cassandra stood, walked over to the fridge opened a beer and handed it to Robert. He thanked her and had a drink. "I think that's enough for now, remember Rome wasn't built in a day," she said smiling. Robert continued drinking, and as he did, Cassandra vanished from his apartment, and Robert again felt very tired. He made it to bed and slept soundly. He had not dreamed of anything except Cassandra since meeting her, and when his alarm rang in the morning he readied himself for work.

Cassandra was correct, humans were an inquisitive species, and Robert didn't disappoint. He was at work, but was reading anything he could find on the internet about aliens. He read about Roswell, and wondered if it was a government cover up or a Huelowen council cover up. He was beginning to get the idea that maybe the internet was the perfect medium for the Huelowen to spread misinformation. Many people believed in previous lives, and he wondered just how far these beings would go to create an elaborate illusion for the humans to follow. These ploys were meant to confuse and misdirect, and for most of the human population they did just that, but for Robert, who had been tutored by a Huelowen, things were starting to make sense. The stories all had some truths, and thanks to Cassandra, he was able to piece together some of the facts buried in these articles. He knew that aliens had been on the planet long before Roswell, and as he looked through ancient civilizations on the internet he realized that the proof already existed of aliens visiting the planet. He knew something that no other living human had ever been told. They never left, and were living amongst their human descendants, keeping themselves hidden in plain sight. He was searching photos of the Roswell incident, and came upon a photo of a person holding what the article claimed was a weather balloon. He was examining that photo, it looked like Roy Summerset. He was in uniform, and looking downwards, but Robert was certain it was Roy, and at that moment realized with total certainty that Cassandra was telling him the truth. The Huelowen had created the flying saucer, crashed it in New Mexico, and allowed the army to claim that it didn't exist. It was a crazy idea, or was it? Robert knew that the Huelowen would go to any length to keep their existence on this planet a secret. He soon realized that with most of the day gone he wouldn't have long to wait. Cassandra would be at his apartment and would soon be revealing more of the hidden truths that he so desperately wanted to know.

Robert was sitting on the couch after dinner watching television when she arrived. He was no longer surprised at her arriving in this fashion, as a matter of fact, he rather enjoyed it. She had materialized not beside him but behind him, and he could sense her arrival even before she placed her hands on both of his shoulders. She kissed him on the neck, and he got goosebumps. He wondered how many people over the centuries actually realised that they were being kissed by the goddess, Aphrodite. She walked around and sat by his side. She had taken his hand in hers when she spoke, "Did you find what you were looking for on the internet today?" Robert now looked like a man caught with his hand in the cookie jar, "How did you know?" asked Robert. "We created the internet as a way to monitor and keep track of humans that ask questions regarding certain events throughout history. Search key words and you will set off our tracking system. Unfortunately when you develop something, it doesn't take long for others to use the same system to hunt for you. Today you were looking at a photo of Roy at Roswell, we aren't too worried about that photo anymore. It's not a very good picture of him, Roy purposely told the reporter to take the picture with him looking down at the balloon. I think you are the only human alive that knows that Roy was at Roswell. Photographs are one of our biggest fears, they allow humans to travel through time and see things and people that should no longer exist. Because of these paradoxes we had to create a whole new set of rules by which we live. We must keep an even lower profile than we did even one hundred years ago. We had to introduce into human vocabulary the word doppelganger to explain sightings of ourselves in old photographs and in other parts of the world. We have even met people years later and passed ourselves off as our own children. It has worked surprisingly well, don't you think? asked Cassandra. Robert had no other choice but to agree, he had no idea that the entire human population was itself alien through the Huelowen breeding program, until he was let in on their secret. He wondered how long they would allow him to live, and why?

The days soon turned to weeks, and Robert found himself living with the woman who called herself Cassandra. She had moved into his apartment, and he could do nothing but love her. She really was Aphrodite, and no mortal could resist her advances. Robert was no different in that regard, but he didn't care. She had told Robert that she had always loved him, and she showed him on a regular basis. Robert was learning more about Huelowen's and their direct influence on this planet. He had no idea that some of the greatest and most notorious were actually Huelowen. Not all aliens, it turns out, were interested in the humans that they had created. Much of the technological advancements were Huelowen to begin with. The Huelowen educators had slowly been sharing knowledge with the human population. They were successful for the most part, but did have uprisings through the centuries that followed. Robert learned that these uprisings resulted in wars. The last of the great wars on this planet had been started by a Huelowen, his name was Adolph Hitler, and he started a movement. He would have succeeded in eradicating all humans if the council didn't somehow get involved. He had gained support amongst some of his dissatisfied Huelowen friends. He himself was bent on eliminating anybody who was not pure Huelowen, but he could only accomplish this with an almost entirely human army to do his bidding. He had captured several

Huelowen scientists, and held their families hostage to get Huelowen technology that wasn't yet scheduled for release. One of the scientists was Wernher Von Braun, he was forced to release his knowledge of rocket technology or his family would be killed. The council had no choice, they contacted four Huelowen scientists living amongst humans in Budapest, Hungary and set them to work on something called the Manhattan Project. It was rather ironic that a human who knew the men coined them as "The Martians." He believed a spaceship from Mars dropped them off in Budapest. He never realized how close to the truth he was. Fortunately, Hitler was defeated, but the technology was out of the bag, Von Braun came to America and humans would eventually go into space, long before they were meant too, and the atomic age ended what many Huelowens referred to as the innocent age of the human.

Cassandra told Robert that it had taken centuries for the Huelowen to discover that breeding with the indigenous biped resulted in a side effect that could not have been anticipated. Although the human body would age and die, the essence and memories would continue. Humans called this phenomenon a person's soul, and although most humans never experienced these previous lives in dreams, it was determined that modification enabled us to not only change skin colour, but also to change form. That scientist touched one of his patients without wearing gloves and immediately changed from our grey skin to brown, and before you say anything, remember that on this planet there are many creatures that can do the same, the chameleon is a perfect example. This allowed us to blend in and take the form of all races on this planet." Robert was now beginning to understand, and the story was taking on a new meaning. This creature from another world, was giving him a crash course in Huelowen history on this planet. She told Robert that they went to great lengths to hide their existence here, so why was she telling him? "I don't understand why you have confided in me," Robert asked, "What makes me so special?" "In your dreams of past lives we were lovers, and I thought you would have realized that I have been following you through time," Cassandra continued, "I can't find you with every new life that you experience, but if for some reason you dream of our past life together, your dreams are like homing beacons for me to follow. You hit your head in that car accident and when you were in the hospital you dreamed of a life with me, we arrived here to make certain that once you recovered that you no longer had these dreams. We found out that humans who have continued these dreams two were lost on the way to this planet. The twelve of us moved to Mt. Olympus, and over time the population called us gods. We were not gods, but our arrogance led to unrest and when the council found out of a plan by the Mayan civilization to expose themselves as Huelowen to the rest of the world, we did an unspeakable thing. The council agreed to use the same poisonous compound used on our home planet to destroy them. In the end all that remained were the buildings, we removed any evidence in that city and placed it in what would eventually become the new meeting place of the council. It is directly under the Mayan ruins, and acts as a constant reminder to the evil we committed so long ago. You asked me yesterday to explain our skin colour to you, and I didn't respond. The first astronauts visiting your planet returned with news of advanced civilizations here, and over the years more ships were sent to gather information. When we discovered that our planet was dying we sent ships again only this time their mission was to gather specimens from each advanced civilization. We realized upon examination that we were not that different, we thought that the inhabitants of your planet, known to us as Man, may have been placed on that world by a distant relative of our own. It was at this time that a scientist working with one of those specimens found out by accident that the gene they did retain some of their previous memories. "People would have a feeling of seeing something before or meeting someone and instantly wondering where they had met," said Cassandra. "You are referring to Déjà vu," said Robert. "Yes, but it goes much deeper than that, when someone says it was love at first sight, it was not, they were lovers in a previous life, but to the vast majority of those people, the memories are just fragments of what was, and will always be," said Cassandra. Robert understood exactly what she meant, he had an ex - wife, but even from the start of the marriage everything seemed forced. He felt different around Cassandra, and was certain that what she had told him about their past lives made perfect sense, but one thing was troubling him. His dreams were different, he dreamed only of Cassandra, night after night. Had she somehow altered his dreams? If so, why? He knew Cassandra and the council was troubled by the recent number of floaters. She had told Robert that the number of people remembering previous lives had been increasing over the last hundred years, and that the council had not found a catalyst. Robert was certain he knew the answer, but would the Huelowen listen. He was set to meet with the council in a few days, and he knew that they alone would decide his fate. He was hoping that the evidence he presented would show that he was worth keeping.

The day of Robert's hearing arrived, and Cassandra took his hand in hers, "Remember, don't let go of my hand until I say so," reminded Cassandra. Robert held on to her hand tightly, and closed his eyes. He found that he didn't get as dizzy if he closed them. They arrived in what looked like a hollowed our cave, and Robert was certain that this was the location that Cassandra had referred to. It took a few moments for his eyes to adjust, and Cassandra had led him to a chair. She told him everything would be OK, she then went and sat at a long table with the other council members. They waited for Robert, and while he regained his senses they talked amongst themselves. Robert could see the Huelowen council clearly now, and was surprised to see the man he had known as Dr. Biggles sitting at the middle of the table. He also recognized Roy Summerset and Cassandra, but although he had never met the others before today, he was certain that he knew each and every one of them.

The Huelowen that Robert knew as Dr. Biggles spoke, "We have all been summoned here at the request of Cassandra, for she has confided in both Roy and myself her desire to wed this human." Robert was totally shocked, was this the only reason for his appearance at the meeting, was she asking the others for her blessing. Dr. Biggles continued, "The human received a blow on the head and after dreaming of his previous lives with her, she was compelled to search him out. She has informed me that this is the life force that she has loved since our breeding program began more than five thousand years ago. Cassandra believes that this man holds the key to why so many humans are discovering that they had past lives, all in favour of listening to this human before we vote, raise your hands." Robert was shocked that the only council member not agreeing was his friend Roy. Dr. Biggles looked at the members and noticing the outcome instructed Robert to speak. Robert was more than a little nervous. He wasn't sure if he should speak his mind to these ancient aliens, he wondered if they would even bother to listen to him. Cassandra smiled at him, and nodded, this was the only encouragement he needed. "Cassandra has told me that the problem has become more severe in the last hundred years, and I believe I know the culprit," said Robert as he continued with confidence, "Motion pictures, they have only been around for the last hundred years, but they have depicted everything and everyone that humans have ever seen or known. Humans don't have to remember a previous life in a dream anymore, they are being constantly reminded of their previous lives through movies and now television." The council sprung to life, and Robert could hear both those who might believe and those that thought the idea was nothing but pure nonsense. Robert continued, "Humans are creating stories not so much from their imagination, but from all the people they have been before. The council knows that human essence is passed from one lifetime to the next, we weren't meant to see these past lives, you have said that yourselves, and to many humans the consequences result in confusion, they no longer know who they are in this life. Some humans believe they are trapped in the wrong body, and will go to extreme measures to return to this previous life. I have experienced only a few of my past lives, but know that I have been an African slave, a white man fighting against slavery, and a married woman who bore nine children, and I'm certain that if I could remember any of the other memories I would find that I have lived an almost endless array of people, a virtual smorgasbord of races, religions, and ideologies. We were not meant to see these glimpses into our other previous lives, and as time goes on I think that you will see more people with mental problems, more violence against others that may have related to some horror from a past life, they won't even know why they hate a specific person, maybe it is some form of payback for hurting them in an earlier life. I don't know for sure, but it's the best explanation I have." The council asked Robert to leave, he would be told of their decision after the vote. Cassandra stood and thanked the council, she led Robert from the meeting room, and with his hand in hers they disappeared, only to reappear in Robert's apartment. She kissed him and before returning to the meeting she handed him a drugged bottle of beer. She wanted him to sleep and not worry about the outcome. He sat on the couch drinking and wondered what would become of him. He didn't have to think about it for long. He was too groggy to make it to the bed, and fell into a deep sleep on the couch. He awoke in the morning and found himself completely alone. Cassandra was nowhere to be seen, and he moved from the couch to the kitchen. He had grown accustomed to having her with him on a Sunday morning. They would have breakfast and coffee and enjoy the time together without having to race anywhere, but today something was different. Robert had no way of contacting Cassandra, he would just have to wait for her to return. He was not feeling well, it seemed to come over him suddenly. He decided to take a nap, and that afternoon he drifted off.

It was a strange dream, he found himself looking up at a man and woman, and they were smiling at him. He could not speak, he tried, but the only sound was a strange gurgling noise. He could understand them, and soon realized that he was a baby. His mother spoke to him as she changed his diaper, he knew what was happening, but he wasn't embarrassed. He could see the look on her face, and he felt her love. He continued to grow, and as he did he found he could crawl around. His mother kept an ever watchful eye on him, and although he could not speak he could understand her. He watched as his first birthday cake was lit and other people arrived to sing to him. The time seemed to pass quickly and soon he had another cake and still more singing. He knew something was wrong with him. Every time he was picked up by his mother he cried. He had trouble turning his neck, it felt stiff, and the light bothered his eyes. He didn't know what was happening, he heard bells ringing and then it was over. Robert awoke to the phone ringing, he picked up the phone and discovered it was a wrong number. He placed the receiver down and checked his alarm clock. It was four thirty five. He had only been sleeping for a few hours, but he wasn't about to go back to sleep now. The dream was fading, and Robert realized that in this latest dream he was a child who died around his second birthday. He grabbed his pen and paper and wrote a few notes. The dream was gone now and Robert could not remember any part of it. Even though he had just finished writing some of the things down, he stopped. He read what he had written, and wondered where it had come from. His dreams had been centered on Cassandra for the entire time he had known her and now with her gone he believed he was again dreaming of some past life. He jumped out of his bed and walked to the living room, he found it empty and wondered whether or not Cassandra would return. He ate a light dinner and afterwards watched some television, hoping that she would appear out of thin air. He yearned for this woman, he knew he couldn't stand to live without her. She did not, however, materialize that evening, and as he climbed into his bed alone he wondered where his dream would take him.

Chapter 6

He was a young Japanese student attending Tokyo University. His name was Kiyoshi Sasaki, who unfortunately had several older brothers and one sister. If he were the eldest son his life would have taken a different course, but with Japan losing the war, he found himself graduating early, and sent to join many other student soldiers at the Tsuchiura naval base. He was to be trained as a tokkotai pilot. He was verbally and physically beaten during his training, as were most of the other young men. They were all placed in a room and given the chance to volunteer for the Emperor. None of the group he was with wanted to look weak, and all volunteered for the assignment. He knew it was a one way trip, and he would never see his family again. The final stage of training was practicing steep dives on the airfield. He would dive straight down, and at the last possible moment pull out of the descent. He would repeat this maneuver until it was his time to make the ultimate sacrifice. He was not a favorite of the instructor, if he was, he would have been sent first. He found waiting for certain death, not knowing when your day would arrive, to be the most difficult. The night before the mission he was given his instructions. The only comfort for him was his belief in multiple lives. He knew in his heart that he would return to his girlfriend. The last letter he sent to her he asked her to seek him out in the next life and the life after that and the life after that, and when she found that person, marry him. His airplane was loaded with explosives and enough fuel for a one way trip. He enjoyed flying, and perhaps in a different time he could have grown old pursuing that passion, but not today. He spotted his target, a destroyer off the coast, and made his move. He was accelerating towards it, and knew the pain he felt would soon be over. He had been hit by fire from that destroyer, but was still able to continue on. He thought of the family he would never see again. He had no time left now, and as his plane smashed into the superstructure he thought he heard bells ringing.

Robert reached over and grabbed at the bells on the top of his alarm clock. He was sweating and dry mouthed. He grabbed his pad of paper and tried to write about his dream. He knew he was Japanese, and remembered being a pilot, he was certain it was world war two. He looked at the paper as he wrote, and couldn't remember anything else. The dream was gone now, and it left him staring blankly at his short note. He ran the shower and as the water poured over his head and down his body he had a frightening thought. If I am dreaming about my previous lives, and that one ended in the 1940's, what will happen to me when I reach my current life? Robert readied himself for work, and wondered if he would ever see Casandra again. He arrived at work, and as the morning passed he noticed that Roy was nowhere to be seen. He went for lunch, and sat alone hoping that Cassandra would show up and brighten his day. He finished his lunch and made his way back to work, and as he sat at his desk he was approached by the office manager. Barry was a fat stupid looking guy with an enormous pair of ears. He was, however, a decent guy, and Robert got along well with him. "I guess you will miss Roy the most," said Barry as he continued, "his mother took sick in Wyoming and he quit last Friday so he could be with her." Robert was initially shocked, but then he knew what was happening, he couldn't say anything to Barry except that he knew all about Roy's mother, but he didn't. Barry left Robert alone and Robert immediately started to put the pieces of puzzle together. He had not seen Cassandra or Roy since the meeting Saturday night, and now they were both gone. He had never been to Roy's place, he didn't even have an address, but he had an idea. On his way out at the end of the day he stopped by Barry's office, Barry was nowhere in sight, and Robert seized the opportunity to search a file for Roy's address. He found it and wrote down the address, it was out of Robert's way, but he needed to see for himself if Roy was there. Robert took a bus to the area, and after a few minutes of walking was standing at the address he had written down. It couldn't be right, he must have written it down incorrectly. He was standing looking at a laundromat. He looked down at the piece of paper with the address, it was the same. Robert had a sinking feeling as he boarded a return bus, that night at his apartment he decided that he would need to do some detective work if he was going to locate both Roy and Cassandra, and he knew where to begin.

Robert called Dr. Biggles office, he had not been to see the Doctor for several months, but was still surprised by the telephone greeting. "Doctor Brewster's office," said the voice. "Hello, this is Robert Marshall, I was looking for Doctor Biggles." "Hello, Robert, this is Nancy, I was Doctor Biggles receptionist, the practice has been sold to Doctor Brewster, and Doctor Biggles has returned to India." Robert thanked Nancy and hung up the phone. Could Dr. Brewster also be Huelowen, it made perfect sense to Robert. He had been told by Cassandra that these pure aliens were scattered throughout the general population, blending in and providing the necessary cover whenever it was required. Robert was slowly realising that he was not going to marry Cassandra or remain in his current life for much longer. The evidence of the Huelowen existence, or more importantly the actual Huelowens he had met were gone. He thought he might find them if he used the information provided, but decided that Cassandra had told him the one thing that would make it impossible to locate the Huelowen. They used misinformation and misdirection to remain hidden in plain sight, and he knew that they could be anywhere. He had one more person to visit, he was the man introduced as Edward Chow, he was a friend of Roy's and if he was at the studio, then maybe he could tell Robert something about Roy Summerset. The sign out front of the studio still had the name Edward Chow, proprietor, but Robert was soon to discover that another Asian was there to greet him. "Hello, my name is Henry Chang, may I help you." "Yes," Robert said as he continued, "I left some paintings here with Mr. Chow, and I was hoping to speak with him, is he in." "I'm sorry Edward has gone back to Hong Kong, he had some pressing family matters to attend to, but let me check for your paintings." The man vanished into a back room and returned with good news. "The paintings you left here on consignment have been sold, and I have a cheque for you." Robert looked at the cheque, it was for more than he had expected. He thanked the man and then asked, when do you expect Edward to return?" The man had an immediate answer. "He has sold me the business, and I don't expect he will ever return to this country." Robert walked out the door and onto the street, and as he walked along he knew that Edward Chow was also Huelowen. It also occurred to him that the man who now owned the studio was also alien. It was the only way any of what had happened made any sense, and he was fairly certain he knew the reason. If these people were virtually immortal, they would need to move locations. Robert guessed if they were not suspected of being aliens they could probably remain in one location for ten or even twenty years. They would never run out of places to live, and then another thing occurred to him. These aliens were probably swapping locations with one another. He had no way to confirm or dispel this latest theory, but to Robert, who was searching for answers, this helped to keep his mind off the missing Cassandra. He arrived home at his apartment and settled in for another night alone. He wondered if he had imagined the entire episode, but a few things were still bothering him. He crawled into bed and set his clock radio to an oldies station. He was hoping that this change alone would somehow help him break the cycle. The lights were off and he could feel himself slipping into that unknown world, the world of another's life, it seemed strange yet familiar to him.

He was at a music festival, and making love to a beautiful woman. He knew instantly who she was. He looked at her face, it was perfect in every way. It was Cassandra, he was certain of that. She really was able to locate him as he passed through time, he remembered the fun they experienced on that farm. He could smell pot in the air, but he much preferred heroin as his high of choice. He had no way of knowing that today would be his last. He was young and full of hopes and dreams, but having Cassandra by his side wasn't enough. He had to have the drugs, after the needle left his arm he felt invincible, and as he lay dying he said to the love of his life. "Do you hear the music?" These were the last words he spoke to her. Robert opened his eyes and rolled over to shut off the radio. He had changed nothing, he awoke at the end of another life, and now as he started to write on his pad of paper he drew a blank. He managed to write only two things. He was with Cassandra, and they were listening to live music at some farm. It wasn't much to go on, but as he showered he thought of something that scared the hell out of him. The dreams had been in chronological order, he was certain of that one fact, and if this dream was from when he thought it was, he was in big trouble. He would check for what had happened on a certain date on the internet, and if he was right, well, he hoped he wasn't.

Robert called in sick, he couldn't trust anyone at work, and didn't know if someone else in the office might be watching him, other than Roy. He turned on his computer, and while eating breakfast he entered his birthday August 17, 1969. He was searching for things that happened on that day, and wasn't sure what he would find, but if his dream was a past life, he didn't have much to go on. The note he had written was all he had. He wrote of being with Cassandra, and listening to live music. Could it be possible that they were together at the Woodstock music festival? The date was correct. The event occurred on what was to be his birthday, and as he checked further he found several people had died there. Could he have been one of those deaths? He had no way of knowing, he looked through photos of the event, but with so many people, finding a photo of Cassandra at that event would be impossible. He had hoped that his dream wasn't a previous life, but now after searching for information he knew the end was near. He sat at home the rest of the day, feeling sorry for himself. He was certain that he had one more dream, and that dream would be his end. It probably wouldn't even matter, he wouldn't remember this life, and without Cassandra here he really didn't care. If she had been telling Robert the truth, they would most likely be reunited in a life that was yet to be. He wasn't sure of his next move, but a thought came to him later that afternoon. He could take uppers, drink coffee, stay active, and do his best not to fall asleep. It was a stupid idea, but he was desperate now. He had nowhere to turn, if Huelowens did exist he couldn't prove it, they had all left town with very plausible stories, and although Robert believed that the people replacing them were Huelowen, he had no proof. The cover stories would not be questioned, they never were, someone else was there to take over the job, and that's all that mattered. Robert now understood how these aliens moved around the world undetected for centuries. He heard a noise in the living room and much to his surprise, found Cassandra sitting down on the couch. "Hello," Cassandra said with a smile on her face. "You're kidding, right?" countered Robert. "I'm sorry I left you alone for the last few days, but we still had some sorting out to do," said a sympathetic sounding Cassandra. "I see," said Robert as he continued, "actually I don't see, Roy is gone, Biggles is gone, Chow is gone, and you, you have hurt me the most," said a not so friendly sounding

Robert. "I am truly sorry, but we had to be sure that you wouldn't tell anyone about us," said Cassandra, "and you have been true to your word, so tonight I am here to give you one small pill, if you take it before bed you will not have the dream that end's your life. It is entirely up to you, but I hope that you will forgive me." Robert took the small orange pill and rolled it between his fingers. "You are not staying here tonight, are you?" Cassandra could see the hurt look on his face, but she still said, "I can't tonight, you must be alone, but I can promise you we will be together very soon." She kissed him tenderly on the lips, and he was hooked. She had that power over any man, but she always chose his presence. She was gone before he could speak, but it didn't make any difference. He really didn't have any choice, it was take the pill and live or not and die. He went back to his room and washed that little insignificant pill down. He felt very strange, and as he lay on his bed his head began spinning every time he opened his eyes it stopped, but it returned each time his eyes closed. He was wondering if swallowing that little pill was such a good idea after all. Robert tried to sit up, but it was of no use, he was pinned to the bed, he had no concept of time. He wasn't sure if he had been asleep or not, his mind was playing tricks on him. He started to believe that time was going backwards, he closed his eyes and the memories of the past few days and then months were playing in reverse. He felt as though he were watching a film being rewound. What the hell was in that pill? He wondered. Finally nothing seemed to matter, and then he didn't remember any of the last few months, his brain had been wiped clean. He was about to start his journey along a new path, one that the Huelowens had planned just for him.

Chapter 7

Robert had not travelled backwards through time, the drug he had been given was a specific short term memory eraser. It targeted only those memories associated with what Robert had experienced since his accident. The drug also allowed the Huelowen the necessary time required to orchestrate the perfect cover story. In the case of Robert Marshall, that meant returning him to a hospital bed. He would have no memory of the Huelowen or anyone he met since being released from the hospital. The drug used was not always successful and in those instances the human subject was terminated. Cassandra hoped that when Robert awoke he would have no memory of her. Some déjà vu was expected, but could always be explained. Cassandra had not been avoiding Robert these last few days, instead she had, with the help of Huelowen foot soldiers, been busy staging a home in the country. They had moved all of Robert's belongings to the home as part of the elaborate plan, and with the home ready, she returned to the Huelowen staffed hospital, ready to proceed. She now was sitting, waiting in the faux hospital room for Robert to awaken. Dr. Biggles spoke to him, and he began to stir, he opened his eyes and asked, "Where am I?" Doctor Biggles smiled briefly at the patient, "You are in the hospital, and had a relapse, you arrived here by ambulance yesterday. My name is Dr. Biggles, do you know who you are?" "Yes, my name is Robert, Robert Marshall, and I was driving my parents to the airport," he stopped and started to cry. "My parents are both dead, aren't they? "Yes, they both died at the scene, but that was a year ago" said a somewhat sympathetic sounding Dr. Biggles. Cassandra had been sitting beside the bed, holding Robert's hand the entire time. He realized this, but not as quickly as one might expect. He turned to look at her, and withdrew his hand from hers. "Who are you?" asked Robert. Cassandra was about to win the academy award, she turned on the tears, and started to sob. Robert instinctively reached toward her. "I'm sorry, I didn't mean to hurt you." Doctor Biggles spoke for Cassandra, "Robert this is your fiancé Cassandra." Robert again removed his hand from hers, and the crying intensified. He had no memory of this woman, she was beautiful, with long black hair and the greenest eyes he had ever seen. Robert thought for a moment, something seemed so familiar to him, but he couldn't quite put his finger on it. Dr. Biggles again spoke, but this time to Cassandra, and as he did he took her hand for effect, "It is perfectly normal for Robert not to remember you, he is suffering from amnesia, unfortunately, his memory may never return." Cassandra, who had the ability to cry on command did not disappoint, she started to cry again, and Robert fell for it, hook, line and sinker. He reached out to her, and as he comforted her, he promised that he would remember her. Cassandra knew that he wouldn't ever remember, the little pill would see to that. Robert had experienced the death of his parents for a second time, and although cruel, it was a necessary part of the plan. Dr. Biggles told Robert that he would be in the hospital for a few days and then he could return home. Cassandra spoke to Robert as she held his hand, "I'm sorry I acted the way I did, you don't need the added stress of me around," she was playing the sympathy card, and it worked. "Please stay, we can talk, and I can get to know you again." Cassandra smiled at both Robert and Dr. Biggles. The doctor told Robert he would check in on him later, and excused himself from the room. Cassandra used this time to fill the vacant mind of Robert Marshall with her own stories of an imaginary life they had together. Robert was none the wiser, and as he listened to her he began to accept the story as fact. They had met and become engaged after the accident, they were living at the country estate left to her by her parents. The estate had a vineyard, and Robert had only been there for a few months before this relapse. Robert listened to the story, and although he accepted it, he had absolutely no memory of Cassandra or living at a country estate. He listened to her story, but at the same time was wondering how he could remember his mother, father and ex-wife, but could not for the life of him remember this beautiful creature. He started to drift off as she spoke, and she stood, reached over him, and kissed him on the lips. "I will visit you again tomorrow," Cassandra said and before leaving she added, "I love you." Robert didn't know what to say. He was dumbfounded, in his mind he had no idea who she was, but he struggled his best "I love you, too."

Robert was alone now, and as he closed his eyes, he couldn't stop thinking of the things he had been told by his fiancé Cassandra. He was tired, and he slept soundly, the drug he had taken the night before had completely worn off, and his dream was of his parents. He awoke to Cassandra sitting next to him, she was holding his hand only this time he didn't mind. He still had no recollection of her, and if the Doctor was correct he would never remember her before their meeting yesterday. He did have the feeling they had met before, and maybe that was all he would ever remember. Déjà vu, he remembered that word, and he knew what it meant. Maybe he had met her before, but to be engaged, and not remember was more than he was willing to believe. Doctor Biggles arrived and asked Robert, "I trust you had a good night sleep. How are you feeling today?" "I still don't remember certain things, I don't remember Cassandra, but I remember the day I married my ex –wife. "Don't you find that a little strange, Doctor Biggles? Robert asked. Cassandra started to cry and let go of Robert's hand, she stood and ran out the door. It was all for show, and as soon as she was out of the room and in the hallway, a smile appeared on her face. She entered a room two doors down from Robert's, and sitting in chairs watching a television monitor were Roy Summerset and Edward Chow. They were watching the feed from Robert's room. "What are you two doing here? asked Cassandra. "Ben asked us down to see if we could jog the memory of your boyfriend," said Roy in a smart ass tone that pissed Cassandra off. "Remember he is going to be my husband, and I don't want you interfering in the project," said Cassandra. "We are not interfering in your pet project, Ben asked us to visit Robert, if he doesn't have even the slightest idea who we are, then you can proceed, said Roy. The two men left the room, and Cassandra watched the closed circuit monitor, she saw both men enter the room. Doctor Biggles was still there and he introduced both men to

Robert. "Two of your friends have asked to see you, I thought it might help jog your memory, this is Roy Summerset, and Edward Chow." Robert looked at both men, he had absolutely no idea who they were when he spoke to them. "Hello, thanks for coming to see me, I have been told by Doctor Biggles that I suffer from a form of amnesia, unfortunately, I have lost my short term memory, and don't remember you two. The two men smiled at Robert, and after having a very brief conversation with him, they left his room and returned to Cassandra. "I told you that he would have no idea who you two were, he didn't even tell you that he felt as though he had met you before." Cassandra didn't need to justify with them anything else when she continued, "he doesn't need to see either of you again." Roy was adamant when he said, "Ben will tell us if we need to see him again, not you." Cassandra didn't bother wasting her breath on either of these men. They left and she re-entered Robert's room. "Two of my friends were here visiting me, but meeting them didn't help with my memory. I still don't remember anything or anybody that I met after the car accident, and that includes you, said a now saddened Robert. Cassandra took his hand in hers, "Don't worry," she said, "if you never get that part of your memory back, we will make new memories together." Robert smiled at Cassandra, and he did believe at that very moment that he had met her before. The door opened and Doctor Biggles entered the room. "I have good news for you Robert," said Biggles, "we are going to keep you here one more night for observation, and after that Cassandra can take you home." Robert was happy and frightened at the same time, he had no recollection of their home, or anything else, and that unknown weighed heavily on his now fragile mind. Dr. Biggles left the room, and again Cassandra comforted him. He felt something for this strange woman, but still wasn't sure what that "something" was. She told him she loved him and would be back in the morning to take him home, and as she left he smiled and with a little more confidence returned the gesture.

Robert drifted off to sleep, and had a dream he had experienced before, with his memory of the last months erased, his mind had been returned to a time of the car accident, and he vividly remembered picking up his parents and driving them to the airport. He remembers them asking him not to stop for a coffee, and that if he did, they might be late for the flight. He remembered telling them to relax, they were going on holidays, and had all the time in the world. He remembered walking into the coffee shop and buying that coffee. He remembered how it tasted as he drove towards the airport, and he remembered the car swerving into his lane. He remembered the sound of smashing glass and crumpling steel, and then it was if someone shut off the movie projector. He awoke sweating and hyperventilating, and realized that he was in a hospital room. Did the accident just happen? He had calmed down now, and did remember being told he had relapsed months after the accident, and was here for observation. The door opened and a nurse entered, "You just had a bad dream, did you want to tell me about it?" asked the nurse. "I was driving my parents to the airport, if I hadn't stopped for that stupid cup of coffee, they would still be alive," said a now angry Robert. "Don't worry," said the nurse, "humans get to live again, and your parents have returned in another life." Robert wondered what she meant, he believed in reincarnation, but it was the wording she had used that got him thinking. "Humans get to live again," Robert said out loud to himself.

The council had met and voted that the marriage of Cassandra to the human Robert Marshall should proceed. The only condition was the removal of his memories of all Huelowen, and that included the memory of Cassandra. The only council member opposed to the plan was Roy Summerset, who believed that this human should be terminated. His fear was that this human would eventually remember meeting the Huelowen and jeopardize their existence and control of over this planet. Cassandra agreed with the terms set out by the council, Robert would be given a pill that had been mostly successful in terminating memories of the Huelowen from human minds, and then she would remove him from his previous surroundings, and introduce him to his new life with her. She knew it was a very dangerous decision, all other humans who had received the memory erasing drug, were no longer in contact with the Huelowen. This man had been shown the truth behind his world, and not even Cassandra knew what was in store for them, but her love for this man's soul was something that she was unable to relinquish. A human and Huelowen had not lived together in thousands of years, and the reason was obvious. They could not grow old together, that was a given, and eventually Cassandra would have to leave Robert, he would die and her search for his soul would start over again. She wasn't thinking of that when she helped him pack a bag and drove him to the country estate. On the way she told Robert that they might be more comfortable in the small guest house, it was the one they lived in before her parents died. In reality the small guest house had furniture from Robert's apartment in it, and Cassandra knew he would recognize it. Robert, of course had never set foot in this house or ever been to the estate, but the hope was that when he saw his furniture here he would believe anything she was to tell him. Robert walked into the guest house and blurted out, "That's my couch, and my coffee table," he ran through the house pointing out things that he remembered and as he entered the bedroom he noticed the old style double bell mechanical alarm clock his father had given him. He took hold of the clock and as he sat on his bed, the memories of his father came flooding back, it felt good for him to remember this. He still had no idea who Cassandra was, and as he looked at the clock he said, "I want to live here for a few days, at least until I get comfortable, would that be alright with you?" Cassandra had expected him to ask that, but she didn't expect his next words. "I want to stay here alone, at least for a day or two." Cassandra understood, it hurt her, but she agreed. She stayed with him while he unpacked his belongings, he was at home here, Robert finally had something he could physically hold and touch. Cassandra had also placed a few of his belongings in the main house, and around the property in the hope that he would accept the fact that he had actually lived here, at least for a few months. Robert walked through the main house, and although he was able to recognize his personal belongings, he had absolutely no recollection of this home. He did, however, believe Cassandra, and when he saw all of his belongings here he knew she was telling him the truth. He did remember his apartment, but Cassandra reminded him that was before the accident. It all was making sense to Robert now, the furniture had been in his apartment, and when they moved into the guest house together he brought his furniture. Cassandra had explained everything to him, and he had no reason not to believe her. He was told by Doctor Biggles to avoid his computer and television for the next month, and although he found it difficult, he obeyed his Doctor's instructions. Cassandra was busy during this time reacquainting Robert with his surroundings, ones that he had never seen before in his life. Robert was constantly drilled with the same stories, over and over again. It was difficult at first, but eventually Robert believed that he had been at this place before, and he began to relax. The country estate did not belong to Cassandra's parents, it had been owned by a number of individuals, all Huelowen, and had been used as a safe haven away from prying humans for the last few hundred years. Cassandra had called it home for only a few weeks, and it was the perfect place to hide in plain sight with Robert.

Cassandra told Robert they had agreed on a very small wedding, and that it would take place at the winery. She also told him that they had picked a date that was important to both of them, Robert's birthday. It was less than a month away, but in the short time he had been with Cassandra he was completely under her spell. The day of the wedding was not a complete fabrication, the minister was Huelowen as were all the guests, but it was a legal union, and that was something that Cassandra wanted. Robert had met all the guests before, but could only remember those he had seen since having his memory erased. He greeted Roy, Edward and Doctor Biggles as old friends and never once thought of why he hadn't invited old friends from before the accident. Cassandra could not have that, she needed time with Robert before he regained his memory, enough time to conceive a child, and nobody was going to get in her way.

Chapter 8

The honeymoon was as well planned and private as the wedding. The two flew by private jet to Florida where they would spend two weeks on a private yacht, away from anyone who may know Robert and jog his memory. The yacht was manned entirely by a Huelowen crew, it had to be for this plan to succeed. Cassandra was certain that this man held the clue to Huelowen survival. She was right, and several weeks after the honeymoon she found herself pregnant. She would need to keep the pregnancy quiet, she couldn't even tell her new husband Robert.

Doctor Biggles arrived at the estate under the guise that he was checking on Robert, but he was really here to see Cassandra. The Doctor entered the study with Cassandra, and she closed the pocket doors. "Can it really be true?" Biggles asked. "Yes, I really am pregnant, but we must keep this as quiet as possible. I don't even want the council to know," said a somewhat cautious sounding Cassandra. Doctor Biggles agreed. The pocket door opened and Robert stepped inside, "Hello Doctor, I thought I heard your voice, are you two talking about me?" "I was just asking your lovely wife how you were coping with married life and if any of your memories had returned." Robert told Doctor Biggles that thanks to his wife he was feeling quite at home here. He still had no memory of the estate but he was making the best of it. Doctor Biggles had Robert sit in a chair, he checked his eyes, and his blood pressure, and said, "Cassandra has told me you haven't been sleeping very well, and that you have been having nightmares," he reached into his bag and handed Robert a bottle of pills, "take one of these every night before bed, they will help you sleep." Cassandra assured Doctor Biggles that she would remind him, she knew exactly what these pills were. She had given them to Robert when they first met in his apartment, and she knew that with them his memory would return, but they also kept him from the progressive dreams that would lead to his eventual death. The Huelowen could not have him die yet, knowing that he had passed the first test, the pregnancy of a goddess long thought barren. Cassandra had told Robert much of the history of the Huelowen on this planet, but she had not told him that the last pure Huelowen child was born more than three thousand years earlier. She wasn't sure at the time of their meeting in his apartment that he was the one she had been searching for, but now that she was pregnant with what she hoped would be the saviour of the

Huelowen race, she could reveal to Robert all of the things she had omitted earlier. She now was able to reintroduce some of the objects to the estate that would slowly help Robert remember the truth. The beautiful painting of Cassandra, the one Robert had painted by memory was hung over the fireplace, and when Robert saw it he said nothing. He stared at the painting, and as he did, a memory came flooding back. He turned to Cassandra and with a flicker in his eye said, "I know who you are, you are Aphrodite, the goddess of love." Cassandra, without saying a word smiled at Robert, it was true she was Aphrodite, and now that he knew it she could tell him the parts of Huelowen history that she had not mentioned previously. She took her husband by the hand and led him to the study. Once inside she closed the pocket doors and sat down beside him. "Do you remember anything else yet?" she asked. Robert looked at her, Cassandra was still wearing her coloured contacts, and he asked her, "you must be tired of putting those in everyday, you do know that you are more beautiful without them." Cassandra stood up walked to a mirror in the study, removed a case from a hidden compartment, and removed her lens. She returned and sat down, she had worn them for so long that she felt naked without them, but Robert took her hand and that feeling disappeared. "I know you are an alien, you told me that some time ago, but I don't remember everything we spoke of. Cassandra decided now was a good time to tell Robert the whole story, he deserved at least that much.

I told you before that we came to this planet and bred with the indigenous biped living here. I also told you that humans were the result of our two species. I did not tell you that around three thousand years ago something happened to the reproductive systems of the Huelowen men. The last pure Huelowen born was a female, and upon reaching sexual maturity was paired with a human who was my son. The hope was to have these two produce a pure Huelowen male, fortunately the child born was Huelowen, but was a female. My son died shortly after that birth and we never got a second chance for a boy. I have been following that essence through time ever since." Robert was paying close attention to what she had said, but he still blurted out, "You mean me?" "Yes, you're essence or in human terms your soul is the soul of my son. I have been drawn to you, as you have moved from life to life. I have watched you as man and woman through the years, and when I saw the painting you did of me, I knew who you were. My son was a skilled artist who was the very first person to paint a portrait of me. I have been collecting these paintings throughout time waiting for him to return, and now I know for sure that you are the one that can save our race. I didn't tell you this before, because I wanted to be absolutely certain, but it was you who painted all of those paintings that I showed earlier," finished Cassandra. "What are you talking about?" asked Robert. "Didn't you just pick up a brush one day and paint a portrait of me, and didn't that portrait look very similar in technique to Leonardo Da Vinci's work?" asked Cassandra. "How? How can you be so sure that in this form, in this body, at this precise time that I am your saviour?" asked a bewildered Robert, it was a good thing that he was seated for what she said to him next. "Robert, I know without a doubt that you are the one we have waited for, you see I'm pregnant." Robert was excited by the prospect of being a father, but at the same time he could not believe it. He said nothing, his mind had gone blank. He stared at the floor for a moment before speaking. "I am your son?" Robert said thinking that he had just done something very wrong. "No, you are not my son, but your soul is my son's soul. Robert still felt a little sick at that notion when he said, "What will happen if the child is human, and not Huelowen?" asked Robert. "Don't worry I am certain that the life growing inside me is indeed Huelowen, but now that I have told you, we must contact Ben Biggles, and set up a council meeting.

Cassandra's pregnancy was starting to show when she and Robert went to council. The entire board was optimistic about the child that she carried, with the exception of one member, Roy, he stood up and shouted at Cassandra and the council members, "This human is not our saviour, she is not pregnant with his child, this is all some sort of trick she has concocted to allow this human a life when he should be dead. He no sooner finished the accusation when he vanished. The council was shocked, they were able to read each other in a way humans only dreamed about, but Roy's thoughts had eluded them. Ben Biggles told Cassandra to return to the estate, and the council would send extra security to watch over them. They must protect Robert and Cassandra at all costs, they all believed he was the missing link in the evolution of the Huelowen people, and needed him alive. They had not told Robert of the life that awaited him if Cassandra delivered a healthy Huelowen. The council decided with Cassandra just entering her final trimester that there was no need to tell him before the child was born.

The estate was now more of a prison to Robert than it had been before. He was allowed in a room that had no door in or out, and here he spent his days painting images of things he had dreamed of. The pills that Doctor Biggles had given him allowed his mind to travel while he slept, not to his final destination, but to places he had previously travelled. He could not remember names, but he did remember homes, places and city streets from centuries gone by. He was surprised by the level of detail he could remember, and it showed in the quality of his work. Cassandra and Robert would materialize in and out without anyone suspecting where Robert was. This was the only room in the estate that no Huelowen, other than Dr. Biggles and Cassandra, had ever been in. Robert knew the reason, no Huelowen could materialize in a location they had not physically been to before. This was how they would keep Robert safe until the baby arrived.

Chapter 9

One morning after breakfast Cassandra decided that the time was right to tell Robert the rest of story that she had been keeping from him. He knew it was going to be a serious talk when she asked him into the study. "Do you remember when you spoke to the council, and told them why you thought Humans were having dreams of their previous lives?" "Yes, I do, I told them I thought people were gaining access to their past lives from watching television and movies," said Robert. "I am now going to tell you the real reason," said Cassandra, "the human mind is now just recycled memories of the past, memories of lives that they have no business seeing. The human mind has reached a saturation point, and now we have a vicious cycle that cannot be stopped. We have tried, but people now hate other people for reasons even they are not sure of. Tormentors become the tormented, and this cycle just repeats over and over, death means nothing to most of these people. They know that they will return, that death is not the end, these people are the most dangerous. They are the ones that have memories, and a false sense of immortality, of a life that never ends, we have tried with stories of bogus holes in the ozone, and fictional stories of global warming. The planet has cycles of hot and cold, and now as we enter the hot phase, we have tried to use this as a means for drawing the people of the planet together. We have failed in that task, and because of this we need to leave the planet. You are the only hope this planet has if Huelowens are to survive." Robert listened, but he did not like anything that Cassandra said. They were superior, Robert knew that, he always had, but what was she saying? The human population was doomed, extinction was inevitable, no there had to be another way. He then said out loud what he had been thinking, "There must be another way, you can't just eliminate humans from the planet, hell, they are your children. You wouldn't kill your child, would you?" Robert asked. "You would if they were terminally ill, if you could help your child die a painless death, I know you would do it." Robert thought for a moment before he spoke, "If you do this what prevents them from returning even worse than before," asked Robert. Cassandra then told Robert the plan that had been tabled by the council. The home planet they had left so many lifetimes ago was again habitable. The compound in the water source had broken down. Space vessels had been prepared for the long voyage home over the last dozen years and the last of the ships was being completed. "The plan had been in place, baby or not. The best part is you will be travelling with us now, we need you to help us rebuild a new life on our old planet," said Cassandra. Robert wasn't sure if she was kidding or not, but he asked her again, "What will happen to this planet when we leave?" "You know the answer already," Cassandra said. Robert could guess, it didn't take a rocket scientist to figure it out, "Nuclear annihilation," he said with no emotion showing on his face. "Yes, it is only a matter of time, without us here to keep our children, as you call them, in line, they will end up killing one another, over nothing more than memories." Robert knew that nothing could be done, and that nothing he could say would change it. He asked Cassandra if it was OK for him to go and paint now, and as he did he realized that he himself was reduced to nothing more than a child seeking permission from his mother. She held his hand and the two arrived in his private play room. He was safe here, and like a child he found himself happy to be painting. The day passed quickly, and that night as he climbed into bed, Cassandra gave him a pill and a glass of water, and kissed him. She told him they would leave this world only after the child was ready to travel. He drifted off to sleep and that night dreamed of working on the pyramids of Egypt. He was not a slave, but a paid labourer, and like his father before him, would spend his entire life working at the site. He saw Cassandra there as well, only he knew her then as Queen Nefertiti. When he awoke in the morning he had breakfast with Cassandra, but could not wait to start a new painting in his secret room. Cassandra was getting ready to deliver, and now a new Doctor arrived and stayed at the estate awaiting a baby that had been thousands of years in the making.

Roy Summerset had a plan and he was able to convince one of the maids that Robert would be the end of Huelowen life, and not the new beginning she was being promised. It took some convincing, but she agreed to his plan, and it would have to happen soon.

Chapter 10

The maid had a job to do, and Roy had convinced her it would be a simple one. She had access to the bedroom of Robert and Cassandra and was originally told to check and see if Robert was taking any daily medication. Roy had been left out of the loop as far as Robert and Cassandra were concerned, but within a few weeks he had his answer. He knew Robert had experienced the progressive dreams earlier on, and that he could not learn of the Huelowen without a drug the Huelowen had developed just for the human mind. It was given a clever name that described its purpose, called the stopper, it did just that, but it could not be taken indefinitely, the long term side effect was certain death. The Huelowen had experimented with it on humans that were on the verge of becoming floaters, it had the effect of returning the drug's user to random past lives they had experienced. The drug was so promising in the control group that the Huelowen believed that this miracle drug would save humankind. The drug made humans less violent, the dreams that they were reliving were all pleasant in nature, and the Huelowen found that because of this, the hatred and anger subsided. The scientists were on the verge of one of this world's greatest solutions. Problems with the drug did not surface until the patient had been taking the drug for approximately six months, and by then it was only a matter of time. The human could continue to remain on the drug and die a horrible death or stop taking the drug and have their final dream. It was shortly after this failed experiment that the Huelowen began to re-examine their abandoned world. The first crew returned with good news, the planet's water supply was now safe. The compound used had broken down over time and was now inert. More ships were built and many of the Huelowen returned to the home planet to start the reconstruction process. The distance between worlds was too great for the mental teleportation to be successful, a few tried, but were never seen or heard from again. Roy had been given the update from the maid working at the estate. Robert was indeed taking pills, the bottle sat on his side table. Roy knew that he must be receiving the stopper drug, and if he was the Huelowen saviour, Doctor Biggles would keep him on the drug to the very end. Robert's fate was sealed as soon as he had the dreams and they used the stopper drug. Roy was on the council, and he knew why they told Robert everything about the Huelowen on this planet, he was never going to be reborn, at least not on his planet. He gave the maid a bottle of pills, they were placebos of the stopper drug. She was instructed to swap them out at the first opportunity. To an outsider looking in, it appeared as though Roy was murdering his best friend, but the opposite was true, he was saving him from a life of pain and suffering. The others on the council would want to keep him alive as long as possible, if only to satisfy their own selfish needs. Roy was boarding a ship bound for the home world, he wanted to be on route when it happened. He met with Doctor Biggles after his arrangement with the maid had been established and requested he be allowed to leave for their own earth. Doctor Biggles was pleased with Roy's decision, for he believed that Roy was accepting the decision of the council. Roy saluted Ben Biggles, and disappeared into the closet.

Doctor Biggles arrived later at the estate and gave Cassandra the good news, "Roy is leaving for earth, he wants to have things ready when we arrive." Cassandra was not sure about Roy, and she told Ben that she wanted security to remain until after the baby was born. "Once the baby is born we will know whether or not Robert still needs protection," Cassandra said. Ben Biggles agreed, he knew by the size of Cassandra's belly that it would not be long now.

Robert went through his daily routine, and he wondered if he would ever see the outside of the estate again. The routine was the same every night for Robert, he had done his job, Cassandra was pregnant, and now he was just waiting for the results. Cassandra gave him a glass of water and a pill, and she kissed him goodnight. Robert felt different after swallowing the pill tonight, and as he entered his dream, it was of a familiar time. He was a kid growing up at his parent's home in the suburbs, he remembered this time of his childhood well. The three of them were together again. He remembered the good times they had, and that they loved him. He found himself changing, he was getting older, and he attended college, and met a girl there. They were married, and then he felt the bitterness of divorce. He moved to a small apartment, and the years continued to pass. Robert was working as a telemarketer now, he remembered that fateful day when his parents died in the accident. He remembered waking in the hospital and meeting Cassandra. He remembered lunches with his friend Roy Summerset, and then he remembered being in hospital again, and then his marriage to Cassandra, and her telling him she was pregnant. The time was passing far too quickly, but Robert had no control over that. He remembered her eyes, one blue and the other brown, he also remembered she was an alien, and that every person on earth was as well. The dream was now fading and he could see a bright light. He remembered people who had near death experiences mentioning a light, but now he was experiencing it firsthand. He had no choice in the matter he was going towards the light, and he was about to learn what was on the other side.

Cassandra knew it was time, the contractions had begun, she tried to wake Robert, but he didn't move. She knew something was wrong with him, but the baby was coming. Doctor Biggles had received her message and he arrived almost instantly in the bedroom. The door opened and others were there as well, the moment had finally arrived, some of them worked on Robert, who was barely breathing. The baby was coming, it had crowned now and soon would be in the waiting arms of its mother. The baby cried, and was quickly cleaned and wrapped in a white blanket. The baby was examined by Doctor Biggles before being handed to the waiting arms of Cassandra. Doctor Biggles smiled at her and she knew that the baby was Huelowen, and as soon as she held him she knew who he was, he had many names over the centuries, but was most recently, the soul of her deceased husband Robert Marshall. She smiled at him, for he was perfect, he even had his mother's eyes. She spoke softly to him now, "I didn't tell you a lie Robert, we will be together forever." He could not speak, he tried but all that came out was a burble. He looked at her and he knew she loved him, and one day when he matured they could be together as the gods intended. Dr. Biggles, seeing that Robert had expired, sprang into action, he had little time to harvest the semen from his now dead body.

It was rather an ironic end to the life of Robert Marshall and to all Humankind on this planet. He was the Huelowen saviour, the one that Cassandra had known would eventually return to her. It had been written in the Huelowen bible for all to read. Our saviour will return with the second coming, and all the evil on earth shall be consumed by fire, and in the end it was.

About the Author:

Robert Mitchell lives with his wife in Ontario, Canada and has two grown daughters. He would like to thank his friend and family for their continued support in his endeavour to create a story worth reading. Thank you.

Made in the USA
Middletown, DE
16 February 2017